About the cover

In June, Harold had preferred Aunt Gloria's newer Navajo blanket with a border. But the events of the summer (of 1958, just before college) led him now to understand and prefer her well-used, unbordered one. Gloria realized this and gave it to him. "I remember the off-white walls in the dorm room…I'll hang it on one of them". **CH 28**

Cover photo by Willard McKay

The Weaving
of Harold Jenkins
By Willard McKay

The story of Harold's summer before college in 1958
during which Harold learned much about life,
death, his ancestry, work, war, love, and
dealing with well meant expectations.

Willard McKay

ISBN: 978-1-4834-3061-4 (sc)
ISBN: 978-1-4834-3060-7 (e)

Library of Congress Control Number: 2015906871

Because of the dynamic nature of the Internet, any web addresses or links contained in this book may have changed since publication and may no longer be valid. The views expressed in this work are solely those of the author and do not necessarily reflect the views of the publisher, and the publisher hereby disclaims any responsibility for them.

Lulu Publishing Services rev. date: 05/12/2015

Contents

Introduction vii

1. Sauve Qui Peut 1
2. Miss Rose 13
3. Gloria of Duncannon 18
4. Nuts and Bolts and Bait and Tourists 29
5. The Turnpike Girl...38
6. Norristown to Germantown..............................47
7. On Memory 52
8. Home...57
9. Leaving Home 61
10. Starting at Gilman's 67
11. King of Normandy 69
12. Lisa by the Road 73
13. Café Society..76
14. Folded Letters 82
15. Garden and Woods 88
16. Time to Say Goodbye.......................................96
17. Of Cars and Bikes: Know When to Fold 103
18. "In a couple of days".......................................109
19. Fourth of July 121
20. A Splendored Thing.. 126
21. Cousins 128
22. "Got it Bad".. 136
23. Unfolded Letters 139
24. Lisa's Back 144
25. Songs in the Rain... 148
26. Peter's Back 153
27. Goodbye Harold 157
28. Unbordered 163

An Afterword... 165

Introduction

Over the years I have been fortunate to meet many interesting people and hear their stories. Some have been happy with where they find themselves, others not. Some have told me how they had changed directions along the way.

I have edited and published two reunion yearbooks for my high school class, our graduation now over 55 years past. They were very well received and brought me many stories of friends of long ago at Radnor High School, a very fine school. There I had a great English teacher. I have named the second chapter in her honor.

I also was an English teacher for a while before going into the antique and art business. I have written many art and antique auction catalogues, and appraisals. This work also brought me many stories about these items and the families they came from,

Later, while staying on Cape Cod for a length of time, I joined others in an excellent workshop for writers, then two more workshops. Those workshops encouraged me. I began work on the story of Harold Jenkins. Harold Jenkins became my main character and then my friend. In my mind he has taken over and told me what to write. In effect, Harold allowed me use of his journal and old letters that his Aunt Gloria gave to him or let him see. It was as if he came to life and wrote this book.

Please consider this introduction to be like the lawyer's disclaimers we frequently read in ads or see on TV. This book may be listed as fiction and shelved with novels. Though the story and the characters are presented as fictitious, that is not really accurate. Many similar or identical incidents happened to someone at some time. I have drawn from these and their lessons for this book. This story revolves around the process by which our lives are woven like a blanket and how we can take what happens and influence the weaving. Or are we simply controlled by the events?

The weaving will be woven, one way or another.

History was my major at Carleton. This interest has continued for much of my life. To the best of my ability, every historical detail is accurate. War and our horrible treatment of Indians are part of our history. Colonel Taylor was real and was reported as saying on Normandy Beach what I quote. Hundreds of Sioux were shot down at Wounded Knee in 1890. Those murders affected Harold and affect us now. The motto of Juniata College is "Veritas liberat." In 1958, a '49 Chevy with a '53 Corvette engine was a "cool" car.

Please read The Weaving of Harold Jenkins more slowly than if it were an action novel. The weaving will be more clear to you. The more carefully you read this, the more satisfied you will be with this writing, especially the last pages. I will have a bit more to say after the last row in this particular "weaving." Perhaps then, you and I shall also have a few questions to ponder.

Willard McKay

1

Sauve Qui Peut

"What is over the next hill?" and the travel descriptions in "On the Road" beckoned strongly. But Harold found Kerouac's writing was too dark.

As he drove his '49 Chevy with the '53 Corvette six engine to his aunt's in central Pennsylvania, Harold missed a turn near Harrisburg while thinking about Miss Rose and headed up along the Juniata River. He had plenty of time so he just kept on the old road. The main route from Hershey to State College followed the river to Lewistown and then crossed the mountain.

It had two lanes, sometimes a third center lane for passing. This center lane was called the "suicide lane". It could be used by people going in either direction. Hence the name.

He tooled along, windows open. For twenty-four cents per gallon he had filled the gas tank near Hershey, something he couldn't often do except for his aunt's generosity. She had mailed him a twenty dollar bill for his trip, just before school let out. He rarely had that much in his dungarees. His weekend and afternoon work in the snack bar paid fairly well and his smile got him decent tips, but it all had gone into the car. It was only nine years old.

The hills seemed to get taller as he headed up river. He figured he would go to Port Royal, drive around the race track area and see if there was anything happening, then turn around and head back for his aunt's near Duncannon.

No one was around. He drove around the lot and rumbled out and headed back toward Duncannon. Nearby was a machine where he parked, walked over and dropped in a nickel and pushed the lever, got his Coke, opened the cap in the front of the machine. As he turned, he saw two local guys looking at his car.

"How come you got duals on that Chevy? Where you from?"

"Up here to see my aunt. I'm from near Philly."

"How come you got duals on an old Chevy six?"

"I got a '53 Corvette six with trip carbs. It needs duals to get the exhaust out fast."

"You shittin' us? Let's see."

Harold proudly unlatched and opened the hood. The two were surprised to see the clean engine with three shiny chrome air cleaners along the side.

"If you get the right parts, it's a bolt-in conversion. You've got to cut the hump to fit and do some wiring. I found a 'Vette where the guy put the rear into a pole. They're fiberglass and the whole thing shattered, but the engine and tranny were fine."

He found himself slipping into their manner of speech. Probably a good idea.

"What'll it do a quarter mile in?"

"About 13.5 seconds. I never ran on a drag strip, just on the Pike back home."

"My uncle's got a '55 Bel Air with two four barrels. Bet he can beat you."

"Bet he can too. I don't have that kind of money."

"You work?"

"Weekends and after school."

"What do you get down there?"

"Buck and a quarter an hour."

"Damn, best I can find around here is seventy-five cents."

Harold eased in and started up and waved as he pulled away, making sure they heard the slight rap of his exhaust pipes. He wondered if there were an uncle with a Bel Air. He was proud to be entering college in the fall. Conscious of differences, he was pretty sure they weren't. He drove a bit, stopped by the river awhile, then continued on his way.

> *June 14, 1958*
>
> *It's like I am free of everything. No one even knows where I am. Coming back down from Port Royal, I've stopped a bit at a pull-off along the*

2

road by the Juniata and I'm just sitting for a while. I shot a few pictures. I hope they come out. It hasn't rained much this June, but the river is still fairly full from the late spring thaw and plenty of rain in May. The sun made me feel good all over like I was a bush growing on the river bank, peaceful between the hills that it flows from on either side. I can hear a few cars behind me on the road, but the rush of the water dominates. I guess I better go. In a different sense than Frost's poem, I have miles to go before I sleep today!

A coupe passed Harold's car and went into the shadow of a mountain as Harold headed downriver for Aunt Gloria's. The mountains threw shadows in the late spring afternoon as he headed east on 322. Really a bit south of east.

Once around a curve, the wreck was almost in front of him. His tires squealed as he slammed on the brakes. "Pump the brakes," he remembered. He pulled off to the side of the road near a car that was over on its right side. The other car had the front end smashed and was spun around in the far lane. The passing lane got them. Harold jumped out. A semi had just stopped, with flashers on, blocking the road on the far side so drivers wouldn't run into the wreck.

"Wish I had flashers," thought Harold as he hurried over to the '50 Ford coupe that landed on its right side. The left fender and side were junk. The body of a young man, the passenger, lay out the right window, caught under the roof. Harold could see movement inside. The driver was on top of the partly out passenger.

Harold almost upchucked when he got closer. From above the eyes, the passenger was missing the top of his skull. His brain showed. A little blood pulsed out, but no movement. Gas dripped from a broken line to form a pool on the road.

3

Someone hollered to the people who lived on the river side of the road to call the fire company. Another yelled to call a doctor too. The woman in the other car was slumped over the wheel.

The semi driver walked to her with another driver who had avoided the accident.

"Kid, give me a hand," a voice said to Harold from near the coupe. "That guy under the car is gone. We'll help the driver."

"He's bleeding. We learned in First Aid class that means his heart is working."

"Kid, I was a medic in Korea. Trust me. You're right, but he's a goner. Maybe we can help the driver in here. Got anything in your car like a pry bar or a big screwdriver? I'm driving my wife's car. Got nothing."

Harold ran to the trunk of his car, got a big knife, long screwdriver, and a tire iron and ran back.

"Good, kid. Now we're going to pop this windshield out."

"I've seen them do that at Haney's junkyard."

They each worked their tools into the gap filled with sealant and pried from top to bottom, then grabbed it with their bare hands and peeled it back, top first, and threw it off the road. The driver was moving, blood on his right arm. He held his head up.

"Whaaat?" The medic reached in and cradled him, one hand under each armpit, with his head leaning against his upper arm and chest. The guy made another noise as his right foot came out. It had a problem.

"Find a blanket or something like that," he commanded.

Harold ran toward the now backed-up traffic. "I need a blanket. Anyone a doctor?"

A fisherman brought an old army blanket and ran with Harold. "What's the story?"

"Bad," was all Harold could get out.

They held the blanket down by the comers and the medic slid the guy on as they got him out of the car. They wrapped it around him, then carried him away from the pool of gas.

4

"When we get an ambulance, we'll lift him on their stretcher with it. They can roll." About then a siren wailed in the distance. Soon a State Trooper arrived.

"You a doctor?"

"Medic in Korea. This one will probably make it, the driver. The passenger's gone. I'll check the other car now." To the fisherman he said, "Buddy, stay with this one and keep him talking if you can." To Harold, "Kid, come with me."

The trucker and another bystander were by the DeSoto. The bystander held a baby in a basket. "The kid's fine. The basket went off the seat, bottom first and hit the firewall and the pad. Kid doesn't have a scratch and is cooing."

The mother was a mess but was talking. She looked like her nose was broken. Tears were running down her cheeks. She wasn't very tall and she hit right into the steering wheel of the big DeSoto. But the metal ring for the horn inside the wheel had broken and she was big-breasted.

"Oh, get me to a doctor. I'm hurt." Looking down, "They're bleeding. I'm nursing the baby. Don't just look at me!" They finally got the door open and she just got out of the car. "Let me see my baby. Is he still okay?"

An older woman came with a shawl and wrapped her up. "I want to go to the Lewistown Hospital. Will you take me?"

"Yes, dearie. My granddaughter can hold the baby."

They left in the woman's car as the cop, the trucker, the medic and Harold watched.

They hurried back to the guy on the blanket as a fire truck pulled in. "An ambulance is coming but it will be another ten or twenty minutes."

The trooper told the fire truck driver, "If you got a radio, tell your ambulance you got a medic here and just get it here, he'll ride in back."

"They got a crew, but they've got to come further. Our company doesn't have a rig." Replied the driver. Everyone just stood around watching and waiting. A local tow truck arrived and hauled the big DeSoto off the road. The cop called for the County Coroner to come.

First a siren was heard and then they saw the red Caddy. Shiny and clean. The driver and the attendant in white got out and looked at the scene. The medic took command.

"Get your litter fast. I got him on a blanket." They sensed the medic knew what he was talking about and wheeled the litter next to the guy. They all lifted the blanket and got him on. Two straps around him, and into the low Caddy that could really run with its big V-8. No one mentioned how much it looked like a red hearse. Off to Lewistown Hospital wailing.

It was a bizarre scene with the ambulance gone and the woman and baby gone. Harold and the medic were on the side of the road, about forty feet from the car with the dead man. A second, smaller fire truck had arrived and one truck was at either end of the overturned car. They had put a blanket over the visible part of the body. Another trooper had arrived and they had traffic moving slowly past the scene. Everyone looked at the car on its side as they passed, a viewing of sorts. A second tow truck waited off the road about a hundred feet west. The peace of the river and the mountains had been shattered.

Waiting was all there was to do. Wait for the coroner. The medic spoke to Harold, "Hey kid, thanks, you did good. Ever been at a bad accident before?"

"No, and I never saw anyone killed. I saw my Grandpop laid out at his funeral, but he was so neat and clean it hardly looked like him."

"You probably won't forget what you saw. There is a coffee joint just a mile east. Why don't we get going and I'll buy you a cup?"

"Thanks, I think I can use it. Started drinking some last year at the snack shop where I work."

From his car, Harold waved to the cop who had said he could go. The cop had their names. The medic got in his wife's Plymouth four-door and they headed east.

A few minutes later, the screen door banged behind them and they were in "Sallie's."

"Just two coffees."

They sat and the medic said, "I'm Mike O'Malley."

Harold held out his hand. "Harold Jenkins."

O'Malley had a drawn face and brown hair, a wiry look. He appeared about thirty-five or so.

"Why didn't you try to help that guy, maybe something?" Mike could see that Harold was bothered by the incident

"I know he was hurt real bad, but...."

"Do you know about Korea?"

"A whole lot of Americans were fighting with South Koreans against North Koreans and Chinese and maybe a few Ruskies flying MIGs. But whoever was fighting, a lot got killed and a lot got hurt real bad. I was there when we took or lost various hills. You've heard, they all had names like Porkchop or Heartbreak and we lost a lot of men."

"We never had enough trucks or ambulances, or buses, or later on, choppers, for everyone. We had to learn what they call 'triage.' They say it's a French term. You got three groups: the ones who can look after themselves, cuts, grazes and the like. Then those who need your help who can be saved, like the driver back there. Then there are those who are dead or going to die no matter what you do."

"You'd go nuts trying to save those who won't make it. Someone told me that hundreds of years ago, when the French found a battle was going to be lost, when they had to pull out, they would yell 'Sauve qui peut.' That means..."

"Save who you may," interjected Harold, a good French student.

"You got it kid. Save yourself and the ones that can be saved. Walking injured helped those with trouble walking. They might carry someone who was conscious. The dead and dying had to be left behind. It is the same way sometimes on the road.

We got the live guy out. The car might have caught fire. By the time we had him safe, the other guy was dead."

"But doesn't it bother you?"

"Every guy wounded, or dead, bothers me, but you got to help who you can and not turn away. You did what you could."

"Yes, but I don't like what I saw."

The medic consciously changed the subject a bit.

"Ever see a helicopter?"

"Just in *Life* and on TV. Why?"

"Choppers. Only good thing about that damn little war they called a 'police action.' They started using choppers to carry guys to the mobile hospitals. Got them over the hills and to the docs much faster. No care en route. Just out there all wrapped up against the wind, but fast. And when we were working after a battle we could hear them coming and we would do whatever we were doing a little faster, so they could fly off sooner. We wanted them to die with the docs if they were going to die, not with us. Only good thing. Choppers. I bet you one day they will have them here and there near bad roads to fly people to hospitals. Just you wait." He even smiled at the thought.

"Do you think it would have helped that other guy today? Maybe they could've put his skull back on like a cap if they could have gotten him to a hospital fast enough. I still can see him lying there. I don't like what I saw."

"Harold, you are a good kid, but you got to know some real hard stuff. When I say 'Sauve qui peut,' it isn't just in a few isolated situations like the accident today or a couple of battles. That is the way life is. You are going to meet lots of people in your life. And you, being a real decent guy, are going to try to help them, and some you can't help like that poor fellow. Some who are alive are going to go on and on about their troubles, but no matter how you try, you won't be able to help them either. Try once or twice, but don't let them drag you down with them. If someone wants help and takes your hand, help them. But if they choose a certain life, you can't make them change."

"I'm not sure what you mean."

"Just remember what I said when you get frustrated some day when you offer a hand and it feels like they want to stay where they are, but complain to you. And don't let them pull you down. And the other thing you got to remember: Don't ever complain that life isn't fair like you think it should be. Life isn't fair. One of the nicest women I ever knew died of cancer last year. Why? No reason. Just died. She deserve it? No. Did she die? Yes. Just remember: Save who you can and don't ever expect life to be fair."

"Life is treating me pretty well. I'm going to college, I have a great car, don't have a girlfriend right now, but that will change. My parents are pretty good; my aunt is neat."

"So what makes that 'fair?' Who says you should have all that going for you? Why not the guy in the car back there? How come he's dead? What was he doing to deserve what he got? Fair to you, fair to him? Kid, I've seen too much. How old do you think I am?"

"I'd guess thirty-six, about."

"Guess I shouldn't call you 'kid.' I'll be twenty-seven in December. I know, I look older. I told you I've seen too much. But I have a good wife. She says I'm getting younger!"

"What do you do?"

"Right now, we live in a little place called Gum Stump. I drive a coal truck up nearby in Snow Shoe. Took today off to go see my brother in Harrisburg. He may have a better job for me. We have a baby on the way and live with my wife's parents. I want something better for her. She is a doll."

As Mike was speaking, Harold had glanced at the clock. "Listen, Mike, thanks for the coffee and talking to me, but I better get going. My aunt's going to start to get worried about me I was supposed to be there over an hour ago, down in Duncannon. She doesn't have any kids and I sort of fill in. She lives in my grandparents' old house up a little valley. I'm glad to meet you."

9

"Likewise, Harold," he said as he got out a dollar and left it as they walked out. Silently, they shook hands and Harold waved to Mike as he drove away, not really conscious that he probably would never see him again.

Harold was still shaken and very much bothered by what he had seen, despite his talk with Mike, and the coffee. He tried to get his mind off the subject as he drove to Duncannon, and his thoughts went to how he got his car the summer before his junior year. Funny, when he had seen the "for sale" sign on the car in the drive by the white house, he had figured he couldn't afford it, but there was no price on the sign. He parked his father's car.

He had knocked on the door of the house where the coupe was parked and was surprised when a white-haired woman, seventy or so years old, came to the door.

He asked her how much it was and how many miles were on it. She ignored his questions.

"Do you go to school, young man?"

"Yes, I'll be a junior at Ridgeford High."

Before he could ask again, she spoke, "What kind of grades do you get?"

"I am on the Honor Roll."

"Do you have a job?"

"Yes, ma'am, I work at a snack bar."

"Here is the key. I didn't drive it much. I got it after my husband Robert died. But I am getting cataracts. Turn it on and see what you think. I only drove it about twenty-three thousand miles."

He got in, pulled the choke, turned the key and pushed the button. It started right up. He drove the pristine coupe back and forth on the drive. Clean as could be!

"I like it, but it is probably too much for me."

"What is your name?"

"Harold Jenkins."

"Will your father put it in his name?"

"I am sure he will, but I don't know how much it is."

"You may buy it for one hundred and fifty dollars and you must pay me at least ten dollars a week until it is paid for, and then you may take it."

Harold started to say "How come so cheap," but thought better of it. He knew it should be three to four hundred. He said "Thank you ma'am."

"Would you like a cup of tea?"

He had never had a cup of tea but knew what to say. "Thank you very much. I would."

They entered a house he later found out was Victorian. It was painted white with shutters and a rounded corner window and a sprawling porch. He thought he had seen something like the interior on a TV show. His family had gotten a TV two years before. Their house was smaller and built after the war.

He recalled the fancy carpet in the hall and the dark wood furniture and upholstered chairs with wooden sides, crests and legs where she had indicated he should sit while she got tea.

He was glad she brought two sugar cookies, too. He really wasn't sure about tea yet. He recalled a story he had read by Rudyard Kipling about a boy who watched the English in India and copied their manners. He did the same.

"You seem like a bright young man. Do you plan to go to college?"

"I hope to. I have to take exams this year. But I always do fine on tests. They are just puzzles."

"The principal and the guidance counselor said they expect me to do well. Dad has a good job, but with the price of things today, as Mom says, it sure would help if I get a scholarship."

"You remind me of Robert. He always had a car from when he got out of the Army after the First War. Actually, he had a 1913 Model T pickup when I first met him. He loved that truck. He would swear at it like a person when he would crank it and it didn't start right up. Then he would fuss with the choke and spark and ask if I had moved them. I never dared touch them.

One day we were going to a picnic and he blew a tire. He had the tools to replace the tube, but he was really a mess by the time he was done. Luckily, the picnic was at my cousins'. They let him get cleaned up as best he could and one lent him a shirt. That was so long ago."

"It takes a machine to change a tire now," replied Harold, "but these modem tires are better and the roads are better and you have a spare right in the trunk anyway."

As he left his memories of getting the car from Mrs. Johnson, whom he later found out was Miss Rose's history teacher, he recalled giving her the last ten dollars he had to his name as a deposit, and then telling his father. His father just said, "Fine, but if you don't pay her off, it's your money you lose. I don't have any to spare." But his father said he liked the car when he and Harold drove by to see it.

Harold's thoughts went back to the accident as he continued. He finally arrived at Gloria's.

Chapter 1.

> "duals": The exhaust manifold has two openings and two sets of exhaust pipes.
> "sixpack": 6 cylinder inline engine... or six cans of whatever.
> trip carbs": In this case, three carburetors mounted on the side of the engine, the fastest six.
> An ambulance corps saying goes, "The Lord protects drunks and babies." (Meaning they are both relaxed.) Use child seats anyway. Don't be the drunk. Their souls are not protected.
> DeSotos and other cars had cast pot metal horn rings. They broke easily.
> LIFE was a magazine everyone read. TV was something some people watched instead of looking at a floor model radio like they once did.
> One of the nicest women I ever knew died of cancer last year." In memory of Margie Stone of Juniata Valley.

2
Miss Rose

As Harold headed West on the Pennsylvania Turnpike to visit his Aunt Gloria, he thought of his journal entry about Miss Rose:

May 11, 1958

Lonely, somewhat lonely. That is what I think of the picture I took of Miss Rose for the yearbook. The light was behind her, and hazy. She was reading something on a desk, standing up in the middle of the room. All alone. I think she was forty-something. She was a bit on the heavy side. I saw a rosary on her desk one day and she put on ashes so I guess she was Catholic.

Somebody said she was going to be a nun but became an English teacher, others thought she had lost a love to the war, but I don't really know. I do think she was lonely. English and history papers were about the only things I did at home or in the library. School never was a problem for me. That's how I could work and fix my car and do other stuff. In study hall I always sat up front so I avoided talking or passing notes like everybody did in the back. I did my homework right after I got the assignment so whatever the teacher wanted was fresh in my mind. I did almost everything else in study hall. I read pretty fast and would even read in class while the teacher was talking or explaining something to someone who didn't get it. I always sat in the back in class if I had a choice so I could read the next chapter or poem or whatever.

I got my car just before my junior year. I know I was spending extra time on it. Miss Rose taught English which I really liked. I read all of my assignments, but wrote the bare minimum for homework. Like when we had to read Frost's "Stopping by woods on a snowy evening." I wrote how I liked the pretty winter woods too, and really liked the poem because I could see the snow falling. I totally missed the deeper meaning of the end: "the woods are lovely, dark, and deep, but I have promises to keep, and miles to go before I sleep." Looking back and thinking makes me feel dumb but I want to write my thoughts!

I did okay B work that first six weeks of fall. I got my first report card. She gave me a C+ in English! Boy was I upset. I never got a C before. I was pissed. I went in to see her at lunch time next day. She was very nice, but said, "Harold, you are an A student and for you to do B work is like someone else doing C work. So I gave you one for lack of effort. Is that what you want?"

I told her, "No. And I don't think it is fair. My average was a B. But you gave me a C+." She said, "If you want to be technical, I knocked you down on participation and effort. That is my job to do. But I am more concerned that you do what you are capable of. I don't want you to settle for less. So I won't just let you slide by. What have you had your mind on?"

I told her what I thought. "I need a car for work. Guys need cars to go on dates and to games and stuff. I got lucky and bought one from an old lady over on Newtown Road named Mrs. Johnson. I have done a lot of work on it and it is almost ready to put back on the road. Cars are really important."

She asked if that were Mabel Johnson and I told her I thought that was the way she signed over the title. She told me that Mrs. Johnson was her tenth grade history teacher and was really particular and smart. Then I realized that was why Mrs. Johnson had wanted to know how I did in school. All of a sudden I realized I had fallen into a little trap. Since Miss Rose knew Mrs. Johnson, she knew that Mrs. Johnson would quiz me about school before letting me to buy her car.

Miss Rose told me how insistent Mrs. Johnson was that they work hard and understand things and how Mrs. Johnson would expect me to do well in school. Miss Rose made it real clear that Mrs. Johnson would be just as unhappy with me as she was for me having let things slide a bit. Man, I didn't have a chance. Then she smiled and said she was sure that this talk would do me a lot of good. Miss Rose said that she expected me to work harder and make a better effort to figure out things that we read.

Then she got really nice. She said, "Harold, you will have a big term paper during the next six weeks. I know how important cars are to young men, but I want to learn more. I want you to write about cars or hot rods or something like that. Make sure you note the magazines you boys read and which are the best ones. I always see 'Hot Rod' sticking out of notebooks. I expect to learn from you and expect a super job in your other work too".

I told her I thought I could handle that. I started paying more attention to what she said and to her in general. I got straight A's from her after that. I even fixed her car once.

Many times when I have taken out my journal to write, I think about Miss Rose who really got me started writing so I written this about her. I expect she will continue teaching until she retires. Ever since I took that picture of her for the yearbook, when she didn't know I was there, I have thought of her both as being alone and as doing what she loves and having lots of grateful students, like me. I guess some didn't like her, too demanding.

Though I don't have her for class this year, sometimes I stop in and we talk. I understand a lot of kids think she is the best teacher they ever had. I agree. She got me to get this notebook and start writing things in it for myself. A journal, but I don't write every day like some people do. I learned a lot from her. I hope I get someone that good next fall at F and M.

June 13, 1958

After hearing about the two kids from North Warwick High, I'm glad we didn't have drinking parties like they had. Just finished school, then dead. The poor guy who was driving lost his friends. I bet he wished he died instead. Graduation was fun despite the formality. I liked the party the way it turned out. Well, school is out now and things look good.

Tomorrow I'm off to see Aunt Gloria for a little while. Of course, Mom plans to send her a lemon pie, as if she can't cook. I just want to hit the road and go somewhere. I am so ready to be on my own. Got everything running right on my car. Half scholarship and work in the fall. Just the way it should be.

Chapter 2.

> "the war" (no caps): The Second World War. Despite the "police action" called the Korean War, "the war" always means W.W. Two.

3
Gloria of Duncannon

Gloria Eberheart was out in her side garden when Harold pulled in by the barn. She pulled a couple of weeds and waved as he got out, not looking the least concerned that he was two hours late. Her brown hair was cut short and just touched the collar of the blue work shirt she wore with blue jeans and work shoes. She had a fairly long, thin nose with a slight forward thrust to it and high cheekbones. Her blue eyes seemed to contrast with her tanned face and arms. You could tell that work did not bother her. She had on small earrings which seemed out of place, but she almost always wore them. People called her a "handsome" woman. Harold walked up and she gave him a hug. "You've turned into a fine young man." Then teasing him, "too bad you're my nephew," alluding to her unmarried status.

"Thanks Aunt Gloria. Sorry I'm late. I started late, then went up the Juniata for fun and there was a bad accident that held things up on my way back."

"Anybody hurt?"

"A woman with a baby was cut some but the baby was fine. Another guy should be okay. They took him to the hospital.... and one guy got killed. It was a long time getting here and I gotta use your bathroom." He avoided further discussion, for the time being at least.

He took the time while upstairs to write some thoughts in his journal and clear his mind.

> *June 14, 1958*
> *This is supposed to be a "journal." I rarely write daily. Les Mots du Mois! I should put more down even if I don't make it daily. I don't feel like writing much after seeing that guy dead. It still bothers me. They weren't drinking or anything.*

18

"Sauve qui peut" and "Life isn't fair." That is what Mike the medic said.

I thought we were in Korea to stop the Communists but he sure didn't seem very convinced. I'm glad there isn't a war going on now. Ike has been there and won. I don't think he, or Mike, likes wars.

As he came down the stairs from the bathroom, he looked around the old house which had been in the family for years. The stairs came straight down the center of the house then the steps turned and came down into the kitchen which had a great big fireplace with a woodstove. The stovepipe went up into the chimney. Aunt Gloria cooked on it and it was the main heat source for the house. Between the old beams overhead was an iron grate where you could look through the floor upstairs. The heat rose by convection. In the winter, if Harold wanted heat in his room, he just opened his door to the hall.

There was a big mantel across the fireplace with old plates of different colors. The room had a couple of tables and chairs as well as two cupboards full of canned goods and such. There was a sink between the door and a window. An old refrigerator with a coil on top stood nearby. An oval braided rug was on the floor. Old stuff, but comfortable. The walls were two feet thick, plaster over field stone.. The summer screen door slammed behind him as he came out.

"I'm over here, Harold," she called from the back of what she called the "house garden." "Come sit with me while I finish the weeding. You need to fill me in on everything you have been doing since last Thanksgiving. Still seeing that little girl from the private school?"

"No, that ended around Christmas. Went our own ways."

"What does that mean, Harold? Tell me about her."

"I met Molly when I worked at the country club one summer but though we talked, I sort of kept my distance. We weren't supposed to socialize with the members. Then later when I was working at Green's Snack Shop, she and a couple of her girlfriends from the Moore School had started hanging out there. I told her they were slumming"

"Slumming, Harold?" interjected Gloria.

"You know, like some rich people going to Harlem in New York. I was talking to my friend Charles about that. His mother came from Harlem; he's colored. She said that white people sometimes get kicks from stopping in the colored bars and night clubs up there. Where I went to grade school the principal would give you hell if you treated a colored kid any different. My Boy Scout leader was the same. I never thought much about it 'til all that stuff that's going on down South right now with busses and school integration.

"Anyway, I told her they were slumming because their families have more money than most of my friends' families do. That school she goes to costs thousands a year. And they still have to pay taxes for regular schools. But she would hang around the counter while her friends sat in a booth. Well one day her friends decided to have some fun with her. She was the youngest and didn't drive. Toward the end of the afternoon they came in, four of them, sat in a booth and had cherry Cokes. Then she came up to the counter and we started talking about Robert Frost, who we both really liked. You know, 'I'm going to clean the pasture spring, you come too.' So two of her friends go out back to the ladies' room and then the other one sneaks out the front after walking over to the juke box. They just left her with me!"

"So what did you do?"

"Well, at first I thought they would be back and I liked it. We just kept on talking. It wasn't real busy, but then Mr. Green came in after he got off his regular job. He takes over 'til eight, closing time. So she started getting nervous that she won't be home when her parents come back from work in Philly. I let her use the phone, but no one was home. So I said I would take her. I think it is just what her friends were trying to set up. Anyway, Molly didn't live more than two miles away. I checked my gas cause it was out in the country. I had plenty. She didn't mind me driving her home at all. Now that you got me talking, I wonder if she didn't put them up to leaving her there!

"I got her home and her parents hadn't come home yet, so we were talking when they drove in. I was nervous, but acted cool when her father came over. She told him 'Daddy, this is Harold Jenkins. He rescued me when my friends played a mean trick on me. We went to Green's but they snuck out when I went up to the counter to get a cherry Coke. I called you but no one was home and I have homework to do. Mr. Green said Harold was a nice guy and I had seen him before, so he brought me home. Please thank him.' He did and we shook hands."

"So we started seeing each other. You know, school dances, a movie now and then, talk on the phone. Some weekends I would have off and go over to her house and we would go for walks in the woods near her house. We behaved ourselves. Just plenty of kissing and hugging. She turned sixteen that fall. Her parents always were civil to me but I got the feeling they didn't think I was quite good enough for her. After all, they belonged to the country club and she went to the Moore School. She and Mom got along fine. Dad was polite but he really didn't have much to say.

"It was snowing one night when we came back to her house near Christmas time. We were in her drive not paying too much attention to anything outside of the car. It turns out her father's boss was parked in front of me in the drive and was waiting for us to get out but we didn't see him. Finally, her father knocked on the car. That made us notice! I said good night. The next night she called and said her parents had decided I was too old for her and we had to break up. I felt terrible, but really knew there was nothing to do. So I hid my anger and tears and just went to the Christmastime parties all by myself. I saw her riding with some other guy that spring, but I had let go by then.

"I never told anyone all that, Aunt Gloria. I just said, 'Oh, we broke up.' You always get everything out of me."

"You wanted to talk about it, Harold. I just listen and let you. Make sure you are there to listen when someone wants to talk. You don't have to say anything, just be supportive and listen. Just be present.

"Was your ancestry part of the problem with her parents?"

"No, she got along fine with my parents. What do you mean?"

"Did you talk about your grandparents?"

"I think she met Grammy once, but you know she is the only one I got left. Grandpop died when I was ten. Your father died when I was a real little kid and I think your mother died before I was born, right?"

"Yes, you're right. Do you know about them?"

"I think your father worked building a railroad or something"

"Yes, and that is how he met my mother. When he was in South Dakota working on the railroad just before World War I. Did you know she was an Oglala Sioux?"

"My grandmother was an Indian? That is cool! How come nobody told me? Are you kidding me?"

"Well, people didn't always talk about Pocahontas or the Lone Ranger and Tonto. Some talked about 'dirty Indians.' Some thought they all should have been wiped out. Some men, very much unlike your grandfather, only saw one good thing about Indian women. Of course, some Indian families looked down on women who married or lived with white men. It was much more unusual for an Indian man to be involved with a white woman. My mother and father just didn't say anything or deal with it. When Mom dressed just like other women, she was a bit darker, but she gardened a lot. She cut her hair in whatever the prevailing fashion happened to be. Though toward the end of her life she let it grow long. That's the way I remember her. I don't know why she changed, but that is how I remember her.

22

Dad was a hard worker and he moved up with the Pennsylvania Railroad and their Enola yards, near Harrisburg. First they lived in Lemoyne, then bought this farm just after the Depression began. This farm was old back then. I think it was built about 1790 and it needed work. Dad worked on it. I got my blue eyes from him! Mom raised us and kept the garden and chickens and cows. He had a job for the whole Depression. Your mother was born in 1915. Me in 1921. Mom died when I was fifteen. She was born in what is now South Dakota in 1889. Her father was killed in 1890, so she never knew him. She lost track of her mother after World War I and never knew what became of her. They weren't close. My Dad, your grandfather, retired in 1945 and died the next year of a heart attack."

"That is so cool! How come no one ever told me before now? Damn, I'm part Indian!"

"Which part Harold? Your heart? Your head? Your arms? You will have to do some thinking about it. But I wasn't sure what your parents had said to you. If your mother says anything, please tell her it just slipped out. So I guess you never told your girlfriend's parents. Well, the reason no one ever said anything was because there wasn't any need to and in some places it isn't 'cool' to have Indian blood. 'Half-breed' isn't a good word. But you are old enough to get married or have a child, so you should know."

"We had a ninth grade gym teacher who's a Seminole Indian. Man, is he strong. No one beats him at arm wrestling. He's about the toughest guy I know. Some guys say he wrestles alligators in the summer. Sometimes our wrestling coach has him wrestle against us. He usually takes it easy on us."

Gloria continued to pull weeds and throw them in the wheelbarrow, most landing in a pile, some falling next to it. Harold leaned on the ham wall just north of the garden and watched her work. He couldn't remember a visit when she didn't keep busy with canning or sewing or spreading hay in a stall, all the time talking and drawing him out of himself. He

23

knew he tended to keep things in. She brought them out. He thought that might be one reason he really liked to visit Gloria.

"Funny you told me about my grandmother. Someone just told me a Lone Ranger story. Lone Ranger and Tonto were riding down a valley. Suddenly two hundred fierce-looking Indians came toward them. The Lone Ranger turned to the right. Another three hundred coming down the hill. Then he turned to the left and another two hundred coming down that hill. He motioned for Tonto to turn around and they saw hundreds more approaching from the rear. 'What are we going to do Tonto?' Replied Tonto, 'What do you mean *we,* White man?' Now I'm not sure who I'm supposed to identify with."

"That's cute, Harold. Maybe you should just do what you always do. Act the right way and allow the people you meet to live their lives. It works most of the time. We choose our destinies for the most part, at least to some degree."

"Do you mean like I plan to go to college so I can get a better job in the future? But what about that guy that passed me then ran into the lady passing the truck? I didn't tell you before, but a guy had passed me and then after the next curve there he was into a lady with a baby in her car. I don't think he, or the guy with him who got killed, or the lady with the baby, chose their destinies."

"What do you call that middle lane, Harold?"

"Suicide lane. Everybody says, 'suicide lanes'. You have to use them to pass."

"You don't have to pass, do you? Those drivers both chose to pass for what they thought were good reasons. They were out there. They sure didn't want to hit each other. But in a way, they got the result of their choices. It was not necessarily what they really wanted. Sometimes life has you doing what you believe is right for you and others. Then something happens.

"Like Pearl Harbor. Everybody knows what happened at Pearl Harbor. 'Day of Infamy.' But the Japs thought they could knock our Navy out of the Pacific so they could extend their empire and hold back what they thought of as our empire moving toward them. Surprise attack, sure, but really, were they going to say, 'Here we come'? Though I just read about a guy who had been a Japanese pilot apologizing for the sneak attack. He was a Samurai, the warrior class. He felt the sneak attack was not honorable.

Apparently, in their tradition, Samurai who had come to attack opponents in the morning would have awakened them and given them time to be prepared to fight, physically and spiritually, not just catch them asleep.

"We lost a couple of thousand good people and lots of ships and it turned out just the opposite as far as what we did. They expected to hold us back, but the U.S. advanced and won. But to some degree, the sailors had chosen to be there, in the Navy, in the ships. It was a Sunday, so some had passes but had chosen to sleep in.

"I don't mean the attack was right. And I don't mean those people deserved it any more than the people in Japan deserved the bombs later on.

"But it came with what they were doing. Our guys were in the Navy on ships of a power seen as trying to take over the Pacific. They got hit. At the end, the Japs said they wouldn't surrender. So the U.S. used A-bombs. Those civilians were caught in something not of their own will, but they lived under that government and hadn't opposed it or thrown it out. So look what happened to them. As for me, I just live my life right, treat people right. Plant my garden and be nice to the neighbors."

"How come you don't have a husband and kids like other women, Aunt Gloria? You sure understand and know a lot. I'm sure lots of guys would be glad to meet someone like you."

"Thanks Harold," she chuckled, "I appreciate your compliment. I'm done; come on in. Time I started dinner."

"You get me to answer your questions, how come..." Gloria paused, then just swept by him leaving him to follow if he wished, and walked into the house and washed up at the kitchen sink.

She turned on her little red radio. The news came on and she turned it down, hearing nothing particularly important. She opened a cupboard and took a couple of potatoes out of a bin, picked up a knife and laid it and the potatoes near him and gave him a container from the sink to peel them into. "I always say, 'give a man a job he can do.'"

She took two paper-wrapped venison steaks out of the refrigerator where she had put them after thawing them that morning. Two years before, she had bought a freezer that she kept in the cellar. It had been a big expenditure, but she put away vegetables and venison in particular. The vegetables were gone, but some venison would remain into the fall. She only hunted in the late fall and winter until she had enough for the year. Her 30-30 and her 12 gauge were in the closet in the corner. Shells for the 12 gauge were above it on the shelf. The 30-30 was loaded except for the chamber.

"What do you plan to study in college this fall," she queried him, having forgotten or ignored his last question. She had finished high school, but never entered college. She read a lot and had taken some extension courses.

"I may change something but I decided to take some more French. I have to take a test to see what level I am in. I have to take freshman math which goes into the calculus. I plan on ancient history, you know, the Greeks and the Romans. I got out of freshman English due to my scores. I'm taking a writing course related to American literature. I could take five courses but a couple of friends in college said to get my feet on the ground first and just take four."

"Sounds great, Harold. There are times I wish I had gone. After Mom died, I tried to look after Dad. You know that little house I usually have rented out on the other side of the barn? Well, I lived in it from the time I was sixteen 'til after Dad died. I was pretty independent, but looked after Dad while he stayed in this house."

"Are you working at Green's this summer, Harold?"

"I guess so. I know it all and it is easy and I get decent tips. I have gotten as much as an extra dollar an hour on a good day so I can't complain. Why do you ask?"

"I stopped down at the hardware store to get a light bulb for your room. I had swiped that bulb when the one in my room burned out. I mentioned to Gil, who owns the place, that you were coming to visit and he asked if you wanted a job for the summer. He and his wife sell hardware, as well as fishing stuff and bait during the summer. Being near the bridge, it gets pretty busy. Lots of cute girls go in when their families come through," she kidded.

"Seems the father of the kid that was going to work for him got transferred and they left the day after school ended."

"I don't know what Mom and Dad would say. They are already saying how much they are going to miss me when I head out to college. Could I stay here, Aunt Gloria? I wonder what he would pay. I have to pay my car insurance the end of the month then put aside money for college."

"They're open seven days in the summer. They open at eight tomorrow even though it is Sunday. Go talk to him yourself and find out. But don't sell yourself short. I bet you can get $1.75 if you will work fifty hours a week."

"That would be eighty seven fifty. I could live with that! I don't always get that dollar in tips."

She went back to fixing dinner. Harold got his bag and a notebook out of the car and took them to his room. He made a bit of noise on the old steps and floors that were just one board thick. He went up and down quickly.

"This house is over one hundred fifty years old, Harold, and I want it to last a few more," Gloria said with a smile.

"Sorry, I'll take it easier. You sure it would be okay to stay here this summer? I don't want to bother you."

"I'd like it. You're as close to a child as I will ever have. I only had to change your diapers a few times. No, I'd be glad to have you. You have to pull your own weight and help with the

27

chores. I won't charge you for food. I always have plenty and give some away. You can eat that part," she said with a smile. "What's that notebook you are carrying?"

"You ready for a long story, Aunt Gloria?"

"Sure Harold, I'll give you all of dinner to talk. You always have been able to talk at the same time you eat! Just slow down and don't talk with your mouth full.

While he ate his venison and then the pie from his mother, Harold told her of how Miss Rose got him to start keeping a journal. After he finished a second piece, they talked a bit more and turned in with crickets and a few little frogs making their night sounds.

Chapter 3.

> Oglala Sioux: Pine Ridge, South Dakota, Wounded Knee, December 1890 (and early 1973.)
> Pennsylvania Railroad and their Enola yards": Major RR pre Amtrak and Conrail.
> Yes, Harold, which part? ..."Thanks to Ed Fell, Penobscot Shaman in Bucks County, PA.
> "Halfbreed": For more commentary see what Cher has to say a few years later.
> "gym teacher who is a Seminole Indian": With compliments to my gym teacher, Chief Metoxen.

4

Nuts and Bolts and Bait and Tourists

Harold got to Gilman's Hardware about eight-thirty so opening chores would be finished, but so the people who got up late would not be there yet.

He followed Aunt Gloria's simple directions. Down the valley road to 11 and 15 by the Susquehanna. North until he saw Gilman's on his left. The first thing he thought when he saw the old brick building with several different style additions was "I hope he doesn't want me to paint the place." It had been awhile since it had been painted or repaired.

Over a door in the largest addition to the right of the brick part was a big sign that proclaimed, GILMAN'S HARDWARE. Other signs indicated you could get keys made, buy bait and tackle, licenses, guns, lawnmowers, pet food and seeds. It looked really old fashioned, but busy. He counted seven cars and one bike pulled up every which way on the gravel and dirt in front and at either end of Gilman's parking area. Another car pulled in as he waited to turn across the road.

He parked and walked in and found it pretty well organized inside with signs indicating different areas or pointing out where to go for the more distant things. One wall in the oldest part had dark oak storage drawers and other containers for all sorts of nuts and bolts and screws and fasteners and nails by the pound and the like. Things with handles like branch trimmers, rakes, and other tools hung above, just in reach. Guns and ammo were in locked glass cases in another section across from fishing gear. It went on and on. A woman who spoke politely but looked tired even at that early hour stood behind the counter near the entrance. In front of her was a brass cash register. People came to her with their finds. A tall, thin, balding man, who he assumed was Mr. Gilman, helped people find things and answered questions about what to use. He helped carry to the counter if needed.

He spoke to Harold after returning from the south end of the building. "Find what you want?"

"Yes, sort of. My aunt, Gloria Eberheart, told me to come talk to you. I'm Harold Jenkins. I might stay with her this summer if my parents say it's all right. I would have to get a job as good as the one I have at home."

Mr. Gilman offered his hand. "I'm Gil Gilman. If you're half the person your aunt is, I'd like to talk. What do you do?"

"Just finished school. Pretty much run Green's Snack shop. Mr. Green has a full-time job so I work 'til he gets off in the afternoon. Sell sodas, make sandwiches; we sell bread and cheese and a few groceries too. Keep the place clean. His wife is really fussy about that. I planned to work there until I go off to college. I need the money. My parents aren't rich and I got a half scholarship but I have to pay some too. I plan to work."

"Gloria says you like cars. You handy with tools?"

"I do most of my own work and help friends sometimes. Even fixed my English teacher's car once. It was just a wire shorting out sometimes, but her garage kept looking for something more expensive. Just put some black tape around it."

"What do you make at home?"

"Well, he pays me a dollar and a quarter. I usually get a dollar an hour in tips."

"Every day?" asked Mr. Gilman, beginning to negotiate.

"I can't say every day, but I do pretty well; probably average about a dollar ninety," replied Harold, also getting into the haggling. "What would you need help with and how many hours would it be?"

"You would have to learn the register, but you would almost always be helping people find things and encouraging them to get them. I would want you seven to four, Wednesday through Saturday, and eight to four on Sunday. It would be you and me Wednesday and Thursday and Sunday morning. My wife won't miss church. She would work with me Monday and Tuesday. I could pay a dollar fifty."

"The hours don't bother me but you don't get tips in a hardware store, do you? I would probably have to get a dollar eighty-five." Harold had spent lots of time in junkyards haggling over the price of parts and the experience had not been lost on him. "Also I have to get my parents to agree to me staying out here in the first place."

"Do you know what I mean by 'add-on sales'?"

"Mr. Green talks to me about that. Like 'Do you want a piece of pie,' or a Coke or coffee with whatever the customer already ordered. I'm pretty good at that."

"Okay, tell your parents I will pay a dollar seventy and give you fifty hours of work each week. You have to start almost right away. If you don't work out after a week, I'll let you go."

Harold quickly decided that eighty-five dollars a week was pretty good and he wanted the adventure of being away from home. "That's fine as long as I get fifty hours. I'll call my parents this afternoon, with phone rates cheaper on Sunday anyway. I don't want to run up Aunt Gloria's phone bill. I'll stop in tomorrow morning and tell you. If I can stay, I still have to go home and get more stuff then come right back."

They shook hands and Mr. Gilman patted him on the back and introduced him to a relieved Mrs. Gilman.

He told Aunt Gloria and asked her advice on how to talk to his parents, particularly his mother. Enthusiasm about a better job offer and the fact that Gloria would look out for him while away from home for the first lengthy time seemed to be the approach. He dialed the operator and gave her his parent's number near Philadelphia. He heard the phone ringing.

"Hi, Dad, it's me, Harold... Everything is fine...No, I am at Aunt Gloria's and she did me a huge favor... She is going to let me stay out here for the summer... Friends of hers, Mr. and Mrs. Gilman, run a hardware store and they offered me fifty hours a week at a good raise from what I get at Green's... About one seventy instead of one twenty-five... It is right near Aunt Gloria's where the bridge crosses the river...He sells bait and fishing stuff too and gets real busy in the summer and Aunt Gloria put in a good word for me... I'd come home tomorrow and back the next day...He wants me to start right away... I know Mom will miss me but I'm going away in September anyway. This way I'll be able to save more for school... I don't know how much, all I can...Aunt Gloria says I can work for my room and board by helping her do gardening and stuff ... Yeah, I'll be home tomorrow by the time you get home from work. I have to go to Green's. I have a couple of friends to send him. I have the week off anyway... Thanks Dad, tell Mom I love her when she gets back. I don't want to talk too much long distance on Aunt Gloria's phone... Thanks, see you tomorrow night... Yes, I'll take the turnpike so it doesn't take so long. Bye."

"How did it go, Harold? Everything okay with being here?"

"Fine. It is much easier dealing with Dad than Mom. He is very logical. He liked that I could make more money and he got it that he can tell Mom it is sort of practice for college with you watching out for me."

"I'm not going to be your baby sitter. You keep things picked up here and help me with the garden, mostly weeding, and that's it. You behave yourself but you are on your own. But watch out for the college girls. Like I said, you behave!"

"College girls, where?"

"Now Harold! I mean at the Dairy Queen and Best Burgers. On the road. They usually have waitresses from Penn State and F and M. You look older than you are, so you behave!"

"You aren't going to make me go to church or anything are you? Mom used to take me but she got tired of dragging me."

"Not exactly. You only have to work in my garden. But my garden and the woods are my church. You can attend if you want."

"I don't quite follow."

"Don't worry about it. Someday, we'll talk about it."

"Last year I wrote a poem about churches for Mr. Sullivan's English class. Want to hear it?"

"You remember it, Harold?"

*"The house of God stands empty in the sun,
among the long un-honored stones of dead.
The silence here speaks new found hope in man."*

"Mr. Sullivan thought it was really good. He often talks about how mankind can improve and that we must improve ourselves. But when I showed it to Miss Rose one day, she just said, 'Well crafted, Harold.'"

"You told me you thought she was Catholic, didn't you? They are pretty strong on the tangible symbols of their beliefs. Your abandoned church image is really not what she wants to hear. At least she was good enough to say what she did, not really put it down. But don't worry; I won't drag you anywhere except maybe to the barber when you need it."

"My hair is not that long."

"If you are working with the public, you have to look presentable. Imagine me going to my job at the county library with my gardening clothes and leaves in my hair!"

"How long have you worked there?"

"Since about 1948, after the war and what it meant, then Dad died. It took me a little time to get everything in order. It's been good for me. I feel I belong. Lots of my friends come in. I'll never get rich but I love to read. I don't think I would like to work in a factory. I know I wouldn't. I'm comfortable. When Dad died, your mom and I worked things out. I got this old place and the money he left went to her to make it equal. She went to school with her money for business courses. I'm happy at the library. I get to talk to kids about books and read to some of the little ones.

"Are they like your kids, Aunt Gloria?"

"Well, I like them, but I don't think I was meant to have kids. I like having time to myself. If you have kids, you never get that.

They are a twenty-four hour a day thing, even for the father. You remember that, Harold."

A thought went through Harold's mind, a memory of something that had stuck when it happened. "Talking about you and Mom, I remember I heard Mom talking to Dad a couple of years ago when they didn't know I heard them. She was talking about some friend of yours with a real good sense of humor. He was from somewhere called Indiantown Gap. Then they heard me coming down stairs and stopped talking. Where's Indiantown? Was he an Indian?"

"I knew a couple of people up there. Nothing to do with Indians. It's a military base they used for training during the war. What was the name?" She asked cautiously.

"I didn't hear," Harold replied as the phone rang. Gloria went into the next room and answered it. "It's your mother."

Harold plopped down in a chair, ready for an argument. He had learned to hold his own and usually won if he were on pretty solid ground and money was not an issue.

"Hi, Mom, what's up?... I know it is all right with her; it was her idea in the first place... I won't be a bother... She already told me I have to help with the garden and get my hair cut...I'm coming home tomorrow to get my stuff then back on Tuesday... I have to work Wednesday. I'll have some time off and will come see you a couple of times, so you can sort of get used to me going away over the summer...And you won't have anything to worry about since I am with Aunt Gloria...Mr. Gilman is a nice guy who works really hard. It will be good for me and I'll get more money for college. Dad liked the idea...You can talk to her if you want. She is right here...I assume I'll have the room where I am staying now, upstairs to the right... (Gloria nodded affirmatively to him.) No... No... I met some people on my way here, when I stopped a couple of times, but I've only talked to Aunt Gloria and Mr. and Mrs. Gilman... I don't know... She was just saying how much she likes the library so I guess she plans to stay there... Want to talk to her?...Okay, I know it is

34

long distance... Okay, see you tomorrow afternoon. Bye, Mom." Harold was relieved.

"She was always my big sister and tried to take care of me growing up. I called her 'Bossy Sissy'. It started because she was bossy and when I was starting to talk I just called her 'sissy' for 'sister'. But by the time I was eight or ten and she was in her teens, I would do stuff that scared her. Like take off in the woods, or catch a jar of spiders and scare her with them. I let the meaning of 'sissy' change. She still tried to be bossy. When she would say, 'Are you calling me a sissy?' I would just smile and say 'You are my sister. I always called you sissy.'

"She was off working in Philadelphia when Mom died. She shared a little apartment with a couple other girls. They lived in West Philadelphia, near Penn, where they worked. I was very independent by then. I sometimes wish we had really been closer. But life has patterns just like a weaving and one row leads to another. See that blanket on the table in the corner with the lamp on it?"

"It's something like the one in my room."

"Very good, Harold. Notice it is very tight but flexible. It will shed water. I got them three years ago when I drove out to New Mexico. I just always wanted to go there. I had read a lot about it. So I took three weeks, one without pay, and drove out to Denver to see a friend who moved out there. Then down over the mountains through a pass that was over ten thousand feet and had a real narrow train track going through it for the mines. I went down to Taos and Santa Fe and over to Phoenix then back through Texas and home. But in a little town near Taos I met a Navajo woman selling blankets and bought the one up in your room. They weave them and sell them to tourists. I must have looked at about every one she had and asked all sorts of questions. It was the end of the day and she wasn't busy and liked to talk. I paid her then asked about her family and 'pueblo' they call it, meaning 'town' or 'group'. She was surprised I knew or cared.

"Then I told her my mother was Oglala Sioux. She didn't know anything about the Sioux except they were from the North, but she looked at me differently from then on. She invited me to come around the other side of the building when she closed up. It was her house. Simple and neat. Her husband was dead, one son had died young, another had been in the war in the Pacific and two daughters were married and had kids. She worked for a cooperative, selling for it. She got by.

"Well, at home she had about five blankets folded up in a pile, similar to each other, and used. They were made the same as my new one but I saw them in a different way. Apparently she had recently gotten them when a relative died and she was the only one left for them to go to in what had been a fairly important family. She let me look at each one in the light through a west window.

"The colors were all natural dyes. No bright blue or orange like in the one up in your room. They showed some wear and the tassels on the four corners were a bit short on some. They were about seventy-five or more years old. The patterns were like stripes and zigzags and such, going across the short dimension of the weaving. I just loved them, and told her.

"Do you see the difference between the one upstairs and this one?"

"It's brighter and not used much and easier to look at. My eye sort of falls off this one", he said, examining the old one.

"Why is that, Harold?"

"The one in my room has a picture frame or border in the weaving around it. It holds your eyes in the middle."

"Very good, Harold. This one was made by a Navajo for Navajos, before they tried to sell them to the white men. Men and woman wore them to keep warm and to keep the rain off, when it came. Some small ones were made for kids or as saddles. They looked at the hills or fields or mountains while they worked at their looms. The land had no borders so they didn't put any in. The white man with fences and yards looked at things differently. So they found it was easier to sell him ones with borders so they made them that way, like the one upstairs.

"She wanted to keep three for her children, but needed money for glasses and to have her old car fixed and would consider selling me one of those she had. I loved this one, simple though it is with the rusty red and ochre and black stripes with a little pattern. She asked me to make her an offer. I thought about what I had to spend and what I paid her for the new one. I offered her twice as much. I think she expected less. Her eyes got tight but didn't show a tear. She took my hand and said, 'Thank you. That's fair.' Nothing more. She gave me some tea and something warm to eat with dark beans. We ate. I paid her and we parted."

"It's nice, but I have only been part Indian for a day so I guess I look at things the white man's way. The upstairs is more to my taste.""To each his own. At least now you know what you're looking at."

5

The Turnpike Girl

Thermos bottle full of lemonade, red cup on top, with a lunch Aunt Gloria had made for him, Harold left after she headed to the library. He threw his bag in back, lunch under the front seat and headed out the valley, up to give Mr. Gilman the news, then south on 11 and 15 to the Turnpike.

Just before he got to the turn-off to the toll booth, he noticed a tall girl hitching ahead. He waited for the light and looked at her. She had a sign that said "Philly." Dressed mostly in black. Black boots, black pants with studs down the sides, black jacket, black bag next to her. Long dark hair with reddish highlights with some curl combed past her shoulders, just a bit wind-blown. High nose and strong eyes, fairly thin. He was unsure whether to stop for her until he saw that she had a book on top of her bag. He figured she must be okay if she read books. He smiled and thought if she were cleaning her nails with a switchblade, he would have driven by. The light changed and he pulled ahead and over for her.

"Where're you headed?" he inquired.

"Philly, my Grandmom's...in...Chestnut Hill. You heading that way?" She smiled.

"Valley Forge, at least. Get in if you want."

She opened the door, tossed her book and her bag on the floor and climbed in.

"Thanks. Got a ride down the river from Williamsport this morning. I go to tech school up there. Grandpop died last year, and I'm worried about my Grandmom so I figured I'd go see her. Thanks a lot. Name's Marion."

"Philly. Going home for tonight, then back out here for a job."

Harold pulled up and got a ticket from the guy in the toll booth. He gunned it a bit as he pulled into the lane marked "Philadelphia and East." He knew he was showing off. He eased onto the turnpike and ran up to a little over fifty, then held it there. "Nice machine. It's good for a lot more than fifty isn't it? What do you have under the hood? Something to go with this floorshift." She patted the shift lever sticking out of the floor.

"Damn, a girl that knows something about cars. '53 Corvette from a wreck. It runs pretty well. But don't worry, I'm not a crazy driver. Got too much sweat and money in it to let anything happen to this baby. You go to a tech school?"

"Haven't you heard of Williamsport Tech? All the different trades you could want. You learn something that gets you a good job, not just a lot of head stuff like college. I'll finish my degree to be a beautician next year." She glanced at her clothes and felt her wind-blown hair and laughed at herself.

"Though you couldn't tell from looking at me. These are my traveling clothes! I generally run around with some guys from the auto mechanics section. I like nice cars. I'll have one someday. I saw a '57 Mercedes Gull Wing Coupe last time I was in Philly. Now that is a car. You can buy me one!"

"Best I can do is some cookies and lemonade. My aunt packed some."

"I'll take you up on that. Haven't had breakfast. You don't have any coffee do you?"

"Nope." He indicated the Thermos and brown bag on the floor by her bag.

She took the inside tan cup and poured herself a drink. "Want some?" He shook his head negatively. She drank some then looked in the bag for the cookies. "You got a couple of sandwiches too. Mind if I have a half?"

"Take a whole one if you want. She always gives me more to eat than I want."

She began to eat the chicken with some sort of greens. "Good. Guess I was really hungry. Thanks. It's Harold, right?"

"That's what they call me."

"How about Har or Hare, they ever call you that?"

Again he shook his head negatively.

"Think I'll name you 'Har.'" She laughed.

"Then you must be 'Mare'!" he retorted.

"Wait a minute, that's a horse!"

She finished half a sandwich.

"Okay, Marion then, 'til I think of something better."

They drove along in a quiet spell where neither wanted to start talking, not knowing the other. They came to the long bridge where they could see the Susquehanna pass beneath them to their right, spread wide and rocky past Three Mile Island, to the Conowingo Dam and on to the Chesapeake, peaceful and shining in the morning sun. Just as they got off the bridge, Harold pulled out and passed three Mack trucks from the same company, hauling coal east. They followed closely like three bicycle racers, two resting some while the leader did the work of fighting the air. As they passed the Harrisburg East interchange, Harold spoke. "Where's your home? Where do your parents live?"

"Mom lives in Danville. She's a nurse at the hospital there. I guess that is home. I haven't had a father since he left when I was four. Twice I've had a 'Tell people he's your father,' but they haven't lasted more than a year or so."

"Your father just left?"

"Mom says he got drafted in forty-two, went to boot camp. He was going to try to be a medic since he was already a nurse. That's how Mom met him. He didn't like it at all. He didn't fit in. They gave him some sort of a general discharge. He came home. We lived with Grandmom at the time. One day when Mom was at work, I was with Grandmom and we were waiting in a ration line. He just packed some things and took off. No note, no nothing. He was just gone.

That Christmas we got a card from him from San Francisco up in northern California. Mom repeats the same story when I say anything. It said 'Merry Christmas. Sorry it worked out this way. This is a place I fit in. It's best for you and Marion.' That was it. If he wrote again, Mom never told me. You sure get me talking, Har. I hardly ever talk about him. Especially when I don't even know the person."

"I think it hurt Mom a lot. She started seeing guys after about four years. We get along pretty well. She did her best to take decent care of me. She talked a lot with me about men. I mean every detail. Much more than most of my girlfriends' moms. My friends come and ask me about everything. I've pretty much been on my own since I finished high school two years ago and went to Tech. I live with a couple other girls. I'll finish this year. I work most weekends and some evenings in a beauty shop. I'll own my own shop one day, or maybe a couple. How about you Har, what do you do?"

"Just finished high school. I'm off to college in the fall. I did pretty well on exams and grades so I have a one-half scholarship and a part-time job when I get there. Right now I'm heading home to get my things and then stay with my aunt in Duncannon while I work there this summer."

"Shit, you're only about eighteen and I'm twenty. I thought you were older. Damn, you're pretty cool, Har, but you're just a kid!" She laughed at the realization.

They were quiet again. The gentle hills rolled by, farms with big stone barns with silos added later. Houses like Gloria Eberheart's here and there. Some Amish farms without electricity or cars. Animals and people providing the bulk of the power. Rickety windmills pumped water for stock.

Harold kept the Chevy moving along now at a steady fifty-five. His friends said as long as you aren't passing everybody, the cops weren't going to stop you for five miles per hour. It made sense to him. A sign indicated a rest area ahead.

"Want that cup of coffee, Marion? Rest stop ahead."

"Thanks; better use the ladies' room too."

They pulled in, used the bathrooms, got coffee and headed back to the car. Two guys on bikes had just pulled into the space next to the car. One on an Indian and the other on a

Vincent. One was combing his long hair as he got off. The other had noticed Marion and was giving her the once-over.

"Hey babe, want a ride?" He greeted her, ignoring Harold who stretched to full height.

Marion immediately turned to Harold, and said for all to hear. "Don't start anything. You know the coach said you were off the boxing team if you picked another fight. Just cool it."

Then to the biker, "No thanks man. I like bikes, but I like his car and especially that big back seat."

Turning back to Harold, "Don't get into it, Har. He's just paying me a compliment, right man? Nice Shadow."

Taken aback, the biker just sort of mumbled, "A girl that knows bikes."

"Later, man; we got things to do," she said as she jumped into the Chevy and slammed the door. Harold got in and started the car with a little flourish of his pipes. The bikers listened and watched as they left, not quite sure of what had transpired.

Harold wasn't quite sure of what had happened either. He had an uneasy feeling of having been protected by a girl. He generally treated people well and simply didn't have confrontations. He recalled a tussle at lunch time in tenth grade, but couldn't remember what it had been about. They got back into traffic, if you could call it traffic at that time of day in Lancaster County.

He turned to Marion, "You sure get your back up. I did my best not to laugh about that boxing stuff, and the back seat...."

"I've been around, Har. Those guys are used to people being a bit afraid and they use it to push people. It might have been cool to go for a ride, but I'd rather be riding with you and who the hell knows where it would have led. I just wanted to give them something to worry about. The back seat bit was to tell them I was with you, not just along for the ride today. I sort of have various plans for when stuff happens. They were nothing to worry about. Didn't need my next line."

Harold, mystified by the assertive girl, asked, "What's that?"

"If one had moved toward me, I'd say something like, 'Sorta hard to ride a bike after this boot goes to your nuts!' Both scare them a little and they aren't used to a woman talking like that to them."

"And if they don't back off, then what would you do?"

"Oh, well to tell you the truth, you should see me scream and run like hell. I'm pretty fast. I'm about taking care of number one."

"Don't worry, I won't mess with you!"

"Well, Har-old, I might like it." Another laugh, then quiet.

They rolled east. Harold slowed as they came to some repair work near the big curve by Downingtown. He just idled along at thirty-five. He wondered about this girl, Marion. She was really cool looking. He knew he was smart, but it was clear to him that she had much more experience in the real world. He had always dated younger girls. He wasn't used to the girl taking charge like she had with the bikers. She must have had some bad experiences with them.

Harold remembered his only personal experience with bikers. He had been about ten. He had been out in the country visiting his friend Jason. Jason's family had moved about thirty miles north of Philadelphia to an old farm. Harold's parents had dropped Harold off for the weekend. It was raining lightly and the kids were outside on a warm afternoon under the canopy of some trees by the road. The road dropped down and made a curve just after passing the house. They heard the sound of bikes decelerating as they approached on the road. Then a brake squeal and rubber sliding on the slick blacktop. And the sound of metal hitting metal, a yell and sliding, scraping sound. Then quiet, then men and a woman yelling at each other. "You dumb bitch..."

The screen door slammed as Jason's father came out to see what was going on. As they approached the road with his father, they saw a pickup truck, in front of it a motorcycle, rear end damaged, lying on the road. In front of all was another bike pulled off to the side. The woman had gotten out of the truck. The two guys in leather jackets stood yelling at her, one with a small amount of blood on the leg of his pants, the other unhurt, both with long hair and beards. Apparently she had slid the truck into the slowing bike.

Jason panicked and yelled, "Bikers! Hide!" to me and his younger sister who had come with us. We turned and ran for the house and up the stairs to his room where we watched what followed.

His dad just walked out and looked at the guy's leg and asked if he wanted an ambulance.

The biker stopped yelling at the woman and pointed to his bike. "The leg is nothing. Look what that dumb bitch did to the bike!"

The three men got the bike off the road and rolled it up the drive to the barn and threw a tarp over it. Jason's dad shook hands with the bikers and one got in the driver's side of the pickup with the woman, the other got back on his bike and off they went.

We ran down as fast as we had run up. "What's up, Dad?" asked Jason.

"Nothing much. They are coming back in a day or so to pick up the bike. Where'd you get to?"

Jason avoided answering, but his sister explained in detail that he had been afraid of the "bikers."

Harold recalled hearing later that the bikers had arrived one night about one a.m. with a truck they had "borrowed" from where they worked at a truck shop. They offered Jason's dad two dollars for his trouble, but he refused it politely, saying they would have done the same for him, and they left.

Construction over, Harold speeded up to fifty-five. The needle on the speedometer had drifted up to fifty-eight when he saw the trooper with flashing lights behind him. He slowed immediately and pulled off onto the first available shoulder. He rolled down his window and waited, looking in the rear view mirror. He could see the trooper talking on the radio, then he got out, put on his broad-brim hat and walked to Harold's car. He was about thirty, brown hair, looking like most other Pennsylvania State Troopers in a neatly ironed uniform. "Driver's license and registration, please."

Harold took them out of his wallet and gave them to the trooper.

"Not quite a standard Chevy, is it kid? You have straight pipes on it?"

"No sir, big legal mufflers."

"Start it up and let's hear it." Harold started it and gently gave gas.

"Okay, but I got you for fifty-seven in a fifty zone."

Before Harold could say a word, Marion turned to the trooper, smiled and said, "I'm sorry; it's all my fault. Can you give me the ticket?"

"What's that, young lady?"

"Well, Harold's from near Philly. He was at his aunt's near Harrisburg. He was heading home. We met out there and he offered to take me to my grandmother's in Philly. He's younger than me and I told him I thought he was cute. Then when some biker started to get fresh at the rest area, I told the biker he was a boxer but I was holding him back, and that I liked his back seat better than the biker's bike. I didn't touch him or anything, but I think some things I said distracted him. He is a very careful driver, but I'm afraid it was my fault that he revved the engine up a bit. So go ahead and give me the ticket."

The trooper had begun to smile. "Tell you what, kid. This is the best story I've heard in quite a while. You're getting lucky twice today. I'll just give you a warning. And you, young lady, take it easy on him and wait 'til he parks the car in the right place!"

He wrote the warning, handed it to Harold, gave Marion a smile and walked back to his car, reported on his radio, turned off his lights and drove away.

45

"Damn, Marion you sure made up that story quick. How do you think so fast?"

She put her hand on his shoulder, smiled, and said, "But I just told him the truth, Har!"

Blushing a bit, Harold started up and pulled onto the turnpike, careful to keep at fifty.

Marion sat there quietly looking ahead or out the window, the slightest smile of triumph on her lips.

Chapter 5

> Switchblade: Popular with cool cats and gang members. See "West Side Story.

> "Thermos brand vacuum bottles traditionally had a screw- on red top cup with tan cups under it.

> "General Discharge": In WW II the only reason this male nurse would get a "general discharge" was if the Army did not want him. He soon left for San Francisco where the Army had discharged others for the same reason. Had Harold figured it out? Marion apparently had not. In honor of my various friends who have found safe havens due to their orientations.

> "Danville": In central PA, home of the highly respected Geisinger Medical Center.

> "Vincent": Vincent Black Shadow motorcycle.

6

Norristown to Germantown

"We're making real good time," Harold said to Marion after they had passed the Downingtown exit, and added with a slight blush, "I mean, I've got plenty of time to take you to your grandmom's. Mom and Dad don't expect me until afternoon. I'll get off at Valley Forge, then take 202 to Norristown, hang a right on Ridge to that little curvy road that goes over to Germantown Pike and you can direct me from there. Okay?"

"Sounds good to me. I want you to meet Grandmom." Marion was quiet as they got off the turnpike and headed into traffic on 202. It was the main road from West Chester, the county seat of Chester County, to Norristown, the county seat of Montgomery County.

Harold explained, "They named this road 'DeKalb Pike' after a general in the revolution. They used to have a big pole, or 'pike,' on a post and it would go across the road so you couldn't drive your wagon by until you gave the man the toll and he would turn the pike. Get it?"

"Like those things you pass when you put your money in for the subway or something like that."

"You got the idea. I learned that when our eleventh grade advanced history class got invited for 'tea' with this guy and his wife. They live on DeKalb. Man, was he smart. He's fifty or so and went to Harvard and Harvard Law School. He's an attorney right in Norristown. He has an office on the first floor of his house, and they live on the floors above. We had tea and cookies in his library. I never saw a person have so many books. Up to the ceiling on every wall. He's a little guy, only about five feet five. Thin. He and his wife ride at Devon, the big horse show and have ribbons and trophies. He's president of the Historical Society and they invite student groups over from time to time. I don't think they have any kids of their own.

"He's funny too, in a real dry way. I was assigned to call up and accept the invitation he had sent our class. I was given the name 'Kirke Brown' and a phone number. So I called and a fairly high voice answered. I politely said 'I would like to speak with Kir-kee Brown.' He replied quickly, 'Since you have mispronounced my name I assume this is a commercial call. Goodbye!' He hung up. I called him right back and said, 'I'm sorry I got your name wrong. I'm Harold Jenkins from Ridgeford High calling to accept your invitation for our class to visit.' 'Well young man, we all are allowed one mistake in our lives. Let that be yours. Thank you for calling. The "e" is silent. Just say Kirk.'"

"When we got there, some guy had been working for him and was just finishing carrying books and files upstairs. We were looking around at the books and antiques and pictures. He came in to get paid. 'Did you learn anything while you worked here today?' 'I sure did sir, I learned a lot. Thank you!' Holding his hand out, Mr. Brown said, 'Then you should be paying me for the day.' The guy's face dropped until he realized Mr. Brown was not serious and received his money. Anyway, he lives just up the hill after we turn on Ridge."

Marion wasn't very talkative as they turned towards Philadelphia on Ridge Pike. Then she turned to Harold.

"Har, look, I can take a bus if you want, but my Grandmom actually lives a bit further in than Chestnut Hill. She is down in Germantown, just off Germantown Pike. If you don't want to go into that area, I'll understand. It's okay. I really appreciate the ride this far."

"It's only a bit further, I don't mind. Why didn't you tell me that before?"

"I thought you would wonder about her and me."

"I don't get it. What are you talking about?"

"Don't you realize a lot of niggers have moved in, Har? It has changed a lot the last few years."

Harold was startled by her word. He did not use it, nor did his parents. They politely said "colored" or "Negro." In Scouts a guy really caught it from the Scoutmaster for saying it once. Charles was a friend of his and had been in the troop, but they never discussed the subject. He just knew it didn't fit in his world. It jarred. Suddenly her attraction diminished greatly.

"Negroes go to my school, Marion. A Negro named Charles is one of my good friends. I am going to recommend him for the job I have had until now. I don't have any problem driving down there, but that is a word we don't use among my friends."

"Sorry, Har, it's what my Grandmom and Mom say and just what I'm used to. They're different than us. Let's say now it's about half-Negro where she lives and she doesn't like it and can't get much money if she sells and doesn't know what to do. She hates them for moving in. She says *she* didn't move into *their* neighborhood."

Harold drove a bit more slowly as he thought. "When Dad and Mom were first married, they had an apartment in Philly near the Armory. Then after the war he used a Veteran's bill to help them move out to the house where we live in Ridgeford. Nobody complained that he and Mom were moving into their neighborhood."

"That's different. They take care of their house and don't make the neighborhood go downhill. And they don't hang around outside drinking. And people where you live know who their father is. Nig-roes move in and it all goes downhill."

He noted her inclination to use the word and her conscious decision to try not to. He remembered what his little cousin Couley had written to him about last year. She was ten at the time, and for some reason they had always talked at the occasional family gatherings. She was an only child and very smart, pretty and a bit pushy in a nice way. Now and then they exchanged cards or notes. She lived way down on the Eastern Shore of Maryland, almost to Virginia. Her family was pretty well off. She and "Miss Bessie," her colored nanny since she was very small, had walked the few blocks into the middle of their little town on a hot June day. Spotting the ice cream shop and having money with her, she led Miss Bessie in and told the keeper that she wanted two vanilla cones, one for her and one for Miss Bessie. "You can eat in here young lady, but *she* will have to eat outside."

"Well, if Miss Bessie can't eat with me, I don't want any." She turned and walked out in a huff. She wrote that she didn't mean any big deal like she had read about at lunch counters and so forth. "It just didn't seem right what he said."

He enjoyed Couley's now-and-then letters and decided he really should write as soon as he got settled at Duncannon.

Silently, they had gotten to the little road across Fairmount Park called Bell's Mills, which ended at Germantown Pike. The quiet seemed a bit awkward, so he turned to Marion.

"What is that book you are carrying? A nything interesting?"

"Har, it's a new version of the Bible that Grandmom lent me. She said I really should study it and learn to be a good Christian. She goes to church every Sunday and often to a Bible study group during the week. I just couldn't get into it. All those families and who begat who. But I'll tell her I got lots out of it and make her happy."

Harold turned onto Germantown Avenue and up toward Chestnut Hill and Germantown. At the top of the hill, he avoided getting his tires on the slippery trolley tracks in the roadway. Once at Germantown High, she told him to slow. They took a left and pulled up in the first block.

"Thanks so much, Harold. You have to come in and say hello. Grandmom will give you cookies, just like your aunt."

She picked up her bag and Bible and got out. Harold followed. The neighborhood looked fine to him.

"Marion, dearie." A voice called from behind the screen door. They walked in and a heavy set woman in a flowery dress gave Marion a hug. Stepping back and looking at Harold, she spoke again.

"Not bad. Is this the latest boyfriend?"

"No, Grandmom, this is Harold who drove me all the way from Harrisburg on his way to his parents' over the river in Ridgeford."

"That was nice, young man. How did you meet him, Marion?"

Ignoring the question, she asked, "Do you have any of your great cookies, Grandmom? I know Harold would love some. I ate some of his."

"Sure, dearie. Come on in the kitchen and I'll fix you something to go with them."

"I really have to get going to my parents, but I do have time for just a couple cookies, please."

"By the way, Harold, I'm Mrs.Turrell. She never introduces me properly."

She turned and brought cookies.

"Thanks very much. Marion, I have to go. If you are in Duncannon, stop in Gilman's Hardware and say hello."

She gave him a quick kiss on the cheek, as if he were a child.

"Thanks, Harold.

Chapter 6

> "Devon": Home to one of the top horse shows anywhere. In Devon, PA and on Route 30, the Lancaster Pike, known As "The Pike," parallel to the Main Line of the Pennsylvania Railroad; an affluent area.

> "Armory": Now home to the National Guard, the area around 33rd and 34th and Market Streets.

7

On Memory

June 16, 1958

I found an old photo after I drove home today, sorting through some stuff to take to Aunt Gloria's. I took the photo on a camping trip. Our Scoutmaster Tim, with Charles, Bill, Jesse and Don. It was Operation Zero in February of 1952 at Valley Forge. He took us so we could see what it was like for the Revolutionary Soldiers. It was cold, but warmed up to about 40 degrees on Sunday just before we left. This was after Jesse chucked an egg and got caught.

Harold thought hard about the day's events as he headed out Germantown Avenue and cut over to Wissahickon Drive, then to the West River Drive where he crossed the Schuylkill River on the old iron bridge and headed for home.

He often thought about memory and memories and how the process worked. Why could people remember things from early childhood but not recall intervening details? Things from various times stood out but he knew he just couldn't ask, "What did I do on this or that day?" and recall it. Themes came up and Marion's comments about Germantown brought up several thoughts as he headed home.

Harold recalled himself and Martin, a Negro boy, had been in the same class for several years in grade school. One day in sixth grade lunch they sat across from each other. Martin made some comment that late September about another classmate, Morris, who was absent due to his Holidays.

Martin ended with the comment, "The Jews are no good 'cause they killed Christ." He was talking to the kid to his left and had his elbow on the table. Harold was upset about the comment of one friend about another. He intended to say something like "Christ was a Jew and anyway the Romans ordered him killed." As he reached out to get Martin's attention, by grabbing his arm, the Negro boy took a swing at him to say, "back off," and happened to hit him on the lip. The lip wrapped around his sharp new braces and he spit blood all over the table. He then found himself defending Martin to a teacher who thought the other had hit him much harder and hadn't seen Harold take his arm. Ever since then he had thought it odd that a Negro boy had commented negatively about someone of another group which also was put down from time to time like his own race was. Harold wondered how it would be for a white boy like himself to grow up somewhere like Liberia.

Several years later he and Martin tussled on the playground at lunch recess over something. Instead of breaking it up, the coach who was on duty let them both get good and dirty, tear a thing or two. He then asked them if they were done, told them to shake hands and be done with it (whatever "it" had been) and sent them sweaty back to afternoon classes. His mother really let him have it when he got home. He guessed Martin's mother had too, since Martin always dressed well, a little more stylishly than Harold. But then Harold and Martin got along well the rest of high school, partly, Harold surmised, since they both were athletic and were on high school teams which got together for banquets and such. Martin excelled as an end on a very good football team. Harold became a good 177 pound wrestler. He chuckled, thinking of Marion calling him a boxer. His wrestling coach got on anyone who got in a fight. He was very strict as to what was expected.

Miss Valentine came to mind, his elementary principal. She treated all with respect and fairness. Harold was sure she had seen much intolerance in the world, but she did not allow it. She was on the large side. Occasionally one of the older boys would call her "Missed Valentine," implying men had passed her by. Harold felt she followed her calling to work with kids.

Jesse was a big boy, with lots of energy, who had been kept back a year. He got into a bit of trouble one time. Harold recalled that he happened to be sitting by the principal's door in the office waiting for a teacher when this Negro boy came in "to see the Principal." He was in Harold's Boy Scout troop. They got along pretty well. Harold was younger than, but as big as Jesse.

Through the glass door Harold heard Miss Valentine speak very strongly to the sixth-grade boy about his behavior. But then her tone changed and she said, "You are a big strong boy, Jesse, you should be helping the little kids, not getting in trouble. You need some responsibility. I am going to put you on the Safety Patrol. You will be at the light on Main Street (the busiest local intersection). You report to me."

Harold recalled two other things about Jesse. One happened on a Boy Scout camp-out. It was Sunday morning and they were about to leave for home. There were some unused eggs left. The trick was to get a guy's attention, then lob an egg high, underhanded, to him. This really got the recipient's attention. He faced several possibilities. If he caught it gently, he could throw it to someone else. If he caught it too firmly, it would break in his hand. If he tried to step back, it would hit the ground, usually splattering him. We knew we weren't supposed to be "chucking" eggs.

Jesse had made a graceful catch of an egg just as the scoutmaster turned to see what was going on. Jesse lobbed it to another guy. That guy saw the scoutmaster, acted innocent, dodged the egg, and it fell to the ground. Their scoutmaster, Tim, said, "Jesse, you know I saw you throw the egg, don't you?" He was known as totally fair when meting out justice.

Jesse said, "Yes, sir."

"Get down and rub your nose in it." Jesse did so without a word. Harold and the other guys knew that Jesse had been fairly treated by his own admission. They were lucky they hadn't been caught. They also knew the incident was over, since if anyone kidded Jesse he would have had to face the same quick justice.

The other thing Harold recalled about Jesse was that he could sing so beautifully. He sang Maleguena for an elementary assembly one time.

As he got to City Line Avenue, Harold's mind drifted to his good friend Charles, another colored boy in the troop, with whom Harold often shared a pup tent on campouts. He was a good camper. So was Harold. By camping together they lightened each other's load by not having a "rookie" or less experienced tent mate. Jesse went into the Navy after high school.

Harold recalled his first real contact with overt prejudice after his sophomore year in high school. Some guys, including his friend Charles, had been playing baseball at the school that summer. One white guy who had money was supposed to have said "Let's all go swimming. Follow me." They got in cars and he led them to the swim club where his family had a membership. Harold worked at the snack bar there that summer. The pool manager told them the "colored boys" couldn't go swimming. Charles and the other colored guys said, "It's OK; you guys go ahead and swim, we're used to it." But colored and white, the baseball players all left, to their credit. Harold had felt like quitting the club job, but needed the money.

He felt he treated the Negroes he knew fairly, and didn't consider himself prejudiced. But then he thought about Betty Ann Jones. With last names beginning with "J" they were often seated near each other from fourth grade on, when her family had moved up from Baltimore. She had been very quiet at first and later confided in him that she had never gone to school with white kids before. She worked hard and they were in the same top reading group. He knew he liked her better than some girls he had asked out in high school, but a nagging something inside had not allowed him to ask her out or even to dance with her at school dances. It bothered him. He hated unresolved questions, especially about himself.

When he reached the Pike, traffic got heavier and he paid more attention to his driving as he headed home.

8
Home

His mind jumped as he got near home. "Home sweet home." "Home is where the heart is." Or as in Frost's *Death of the Hired Man*, "Home is where, when you have to go there, they have to take you in."

Everything would be fine with his father. He would tell Harold to work hard, pay attention to Mr. Gilman and be respectful of his Aunt Gloria, only he would say, "your mother's sister Gloria." His mother would be difficult.

She would rush around trying to get everything he would need while at the same time saying "Do you really want to go?" "I'm going to miss you." "What if you don't get along with Mr. Gilman?" She just had to say things. She really didn't want his responses or answers to thoughts posed as questions. He knew he would to bed, then leave in the morning.

Finally home, he parked out front. His father wasn't home yet, so he was careful not to block the drive.

His mother, in her familiar grey skirt and white blouse, came out of the front door before he got out of the car, as if she had been waiting at a window for his arrival. She came around to his side of the car and gave him a hug as he got out. "I am so glad you got here all right. It's such a long drive from Gloria's. You made very good time. Come on in, I have a sandwich waiting for you."

Harold gave her his best smile. He had already decided not to mention giving Marion a ride. The whole thing was too complicated. They headed across the yard. "I guess Dad told you it's a real good job I have for the summer."

"I'm sure it is, Harold. I just wonder if you really are ready to be away. I thought we would have a lot of time to talk this summer. Are you sure you want to stay out there? You don't know anyone but Aunt Gloria. Won't you miss your friends?"

"I'll be fine, Mom. It is really a good idea. I will be pretty much on my own, like being at college, and I'll come back home a couple of times. It will be fine. And I'll get used to being away without having to work on my classes at the same time. In a way I'll have the advantage over other kids this fall. They will be homesick and worried about their studies at the same time. I won't." He patted her on the shoulder as they walked in, realizing that it was she who would miss him and wanted to talk with him. He talked more easily with his aunt, but then she was younger and not in charge of him like his mother was.

"I have a sandwich and some lemonade for you. Did Gloria give you anything?"

"Yeah, but I'm hungry. It was sort of breakfast. Show me the food!" Lettuce and tomato and mayonnaise with thinly sliced Spam on fluffy white bread. He ate quickly and asked for a second glass of lemonade, which pleased his mother. She took the time to squeeze lemons and make it fresh.

"I have to run over and tell Mr. Green. I have a couple of friends who are looking for jobs so he won't have a problem finding someone."

"Can't you sit just a bit and talk? I want to hear about your trip and how Gloria is."

"Okay Mom, I'll sit for a little before I go." He reported that Gloria was well, and the prospective job challenging and interesting. The trip part lacked some detail. Then he left for Green's. He gave Mr. Green the news with the emphasis on wanting to work away from home to get used to being away before attending college and gave him Charles' phone number and some other names and numbers. Mr. Green had the week off from his regular job, so he was working the whole day anyway. Mr. Green asked him not to tell his friends what he was making. Harold assumed Mr. Green hoped to start someone at less than what he paid Harold. Harold agreed. They shook hands and Harold left and drove around town, looking at it for a last time before going to Aunt Gloria's.

It was sort of a self-guided tour he realized. He lived fairly close to the elementary school he had attended and he pulled into the vacant bus drive when he got there. School was out. No one was around. He glanced at the playfields around the building and the worn area near bushes and a sandbox where, as an older kid, he had taken part in "chicken fights" where one guy rode the waist of a bigger kid, holding on with legs tight and one hand on the shoulder and another outstretched to catch the opposing rider. The chicken held his arms tight in around the rider's legs. Their rules forbade his using his hands to grab the other. The pair whose rider fell off or went down were the losers. Strangely disciplined. No scratching or poking eyes was allowed. One chicken couldn't step on the other chicken's feet.

Harold's eyes moved up to the sixth-grade room. No papers or decorations of any sort left in the windows. He remembered it as always having something kids had done up on the walls or windows. Harold had read everything he could once he got started. He had been told he was "late," not reading much until second grade. Once he got going he always had a book with him. To reward readers, the sixth-grade teacher, Mr. Orlando, had students give him verbal or written book reports each time they finished a book. Then if Mr. Orlando were satisfied, he would put a piece of construction paper on a chart as wide as the thickness of the book with the name of the book written on it. The idea was to reward readers and to let others see the names of books their peers had enjoyed. The kidding began when Harold's bar was about fifty percent longer than anyone else's. By the time it was close to twice the length, Harold got tired of the kidding and stopped reporting. He kept on reading and just let others catch up. He was competitive enough that when others finally caught up he turned in a report or two so he stayed ahead. Mr. Orlando never said anything. Now, Harold realized, Mr. Orlando had been smart enough to have figured out what was going on.

Before leaving, his eyes drifted to the front door and his mind to memories of Miss Valentine, whose office was down the hall.

It was a sunny afternoon, starting to warm up for summer. As he cut off on a winding little road he watched his speed. The word was that since a big-wig lived on a farm he would soon pass, the township police frequently hid and enforced the 30 MPH limit that was posted. All Harold's friends felt it should be 40 or 45, but they knew to be careful. He glanced up on the hillside and smiled at the herd of cows, standing still in the sun.

Carefully he turned onto the little dirt road to the creek and pulled off where it widened. Another car was further down the road. He got out and walked toward the creek where he saw a guy fishing with his two kids. One yanked a three-inch sunny out of the water then wanted to take it home for dinner. The father insisted that it be released "to grow up and be big enough to eat."

Harold walked up a bit, through the old iron fence, and sat on a familiar rock overlooking the creek, a dam and a little glen. Bittersweet thoughts of leaving filled his mind. He left and walked back to his car and headed for town.

9

Leaving Home

No cops, no hitchhikers in black. The trip back to Duncannon was uneventful. The evening before had been the same. Home for dinner with his parents, he reviewed his plans, promised to visit a couple of times. Then he packed his car, slept, had a nice breakfast and headed down the Turnpike to Harrisburg. Just a quick ride back to Aunt Gloria's.

He crossed the river, this time looking north at the islands and people fishing here and there, probably for bass at this time of the year.

He got off the Turnpike and paid. As he went down the ramp he hit a pothole as he was looking to merge onto the north-bound lane. Everything felt fine but he had heard a noise in the back seat and realized his black Zenith radio had shifted. No damage though. He went towards Duncannon. The sound made him aware of how much he had loaded into the car. He had most of his stuff, except for books he had read still on his shelf, and some car parts in the basement and his heavier winter clothes that were packed in a trunk in the attic or on hangers in his closet. It suddenly dawned on him that in a sense he had really left home.

The thought didn't bother him at all. It was something he had been planning to do, and it just happened a bit sooner than he had planned. Since April when the guidance department at Ridgeford had offered a program with two sessions taken out of study halls especially for college-bound seniors on the subject of leaving home. It had irritated him a bit since he used his study halls well so that he could do his work almost entirely in school, thus allowing for work and other interests.

Apparently some kids had a hard time when they went away to school. They weren't used to organizing their time for themselves so they didn't spend enough time on schoolwork. The counselors had talked about how too much time might get spent on social life either in the sense of chasing girls or drinking with friends. Harold and his friends drank a little beer now and then when someone somehow got some, but not to excess. Usually one guy got a six-pack and four or five drank it. He was used to having a girlfriend and those he had dated had liked having a studious guy who also happened to be athletic and had a nice car. He knew how to prevent getting a girl pregnant. He really wasn't very concerned about leaving home.

He recalled in the second hour of the guidance program that they had mentioned it might be hard on some parents to let go. He remembered a friend having a little book by Gibran called *The Prophet* by Gibran that he had borrowed last year. "Your children are not your children. They are the sons and daughters of life's longing for itself" or something like that. It too implied that parents had trouble allowing children to go off and live their lives.

He wondered about his mother. She used to drive him to practices and parties when he was younger. She still insisted on going with him to buy clothes. He wondered if she would go back to the office work she used to do. Harold had a troubling thought, but he knew it was true. There were a couple of teachers he knew and one woman who came into Green's that he really liked and spent time talking with. Harold regarded them as friends, but they were considerably older than he. He realized that if he were not his mother's son, he probably would not include his mother among this group of "older friends." He realized he probably would not include his father either. He was bothered, but he knew it was so.

Harold decided he would send his mother a nice card in a couple of days and tell her what a good mother she was and how much he appreciated her. She could show it to her friends. He continued to Aunt Gloria's and began thinking about her.

It suddenly occurred to him that Gloria fit into his "older friends" category. Sure, he was related to her, and she was older and spoke from more experience, but she related differently to him. He thought about it and realized she didn't have to be tied to what she said. Like the Navajo rugs. It was okay with her that he preferred the new one with borders. He didn't have to have the same religious thoughts or practices as she. She made him feel welcome and told him what she expected if he were staying with her, but it wasn't like it was the "right way" to do things. It was her house and it was sort of a business deal "if you want this, I expect that." Too bad she didn't have kids. She would be a good mother. Then he thought again about the fact that she was single at thirty-eight. Whenever he brought it up she avoided his question. It was like walking into a wire-mesh fence that wasn't too tight between the posts. You just gently bounced off. He had a feeling that there was a very long story that he would eventually hear. He recalled hearing someone say "we learn most from love and pain" and sensed that these both had something to do with her story.

He entered Aunt Gloria's drive and a new stage of his life. There was a fifty-seven Pontiac station wagon in the driveway that he did not recognize. He saw Aunt Gloria over at the little house coming out of the front door followed by a tall man, graying at the temples, who walked with a slight limp and a cane. They came toward Harold.

"Mr. King, this is my nephew Harold from near Philadelphia."

"Harold, this is Mr. Peter King. He may rent the little house. He is the new assistant superintendent of schools in the area."

Harold and Peter shook hands. Harold noted that despite his cane, he had a strong grip. They walked toward the house.

Peter spoke. "I am almost sure I want the place. I would like to call tomorrow night if you can wait that long for a final answer. One thing though: I prefer 'Pete.' Mr. King was my father!"

"And I'm Gloria," she said with a slight smile. Harold followed her inside as "Pete" walked to his car and left.

"Had lunch?"

"Hoped you'd ask!" Harold put his bag down, saw trash ready to go out, took it to the burn pile and came back in.

"Bill Keller, the high school principal, stopped in yesterday and asked if I wanted to rent the little house. I decided it was a good time with you here this summer. In case there were any problem with a new person. I knew you would watch over me," she said half seriously, half teasingly.

"I'm sure he will be fine, Aunt Gloria. An assistant superintendent. I know the school board really checks out people back home. Two years ago there was a big ruckus over a new superintendent, but things calmed down and he stayed.

"That was cute about me here to watch over you, Aunt Gloria, but somehow I think you can take pretty good care of yourself. I think that is why I always liked you. Mom is nice but she really leans on Dad. I guess she could get by fine if something happened to him, but though she talks a lot, he really makes all the major decisions. Many of the girls I know, and I mean ones with brains, spend their time planning how to look and dress to catch some guy. I know a couple of girls who were in our academic classes who went down to general after tenth so they didn't have to spend any time on schoolwork. All they want is eventually to get married and have a kid."

"Well Harold, you seem to think that is what women are supposed to do."

"No, I don't; people ought to do what they like."

"Oh, then how come you comment on the fact I'm single? Don't you think the attitudes held by you and the other guys have an effect on those girls, besides their families and all?"

Families. friends and others around us seem to have what I call 'well-meaning expectations', which are not necessarily in our best interest.'"

"You sort of say, 'Hey girl, you ought to get married, look at me.' And they play up to you."

"You got me, Aunt Gloria you just led me down the path like the debate coach said to do. I think part of me says one thing and my mind says another."

"So now that you are conscious of it, think about it and decide how you want to act."

"What do you want for lunch?"

"Just anything, thanks. I know you have to get back to work. What is this King guy like?"

"I guess he's a pretty good guy if he is going to be the assistant superintendent. I think from what Bill Keller said that he was injured on D-Day at Normandy. Mr. King didn't say anything about it to me. He has a master's degree, Bill said. He's polite and reserved."

"You like him?"

"I think he'll be an honest and quiet tenant."

Harold decided to leave it alone. He knew Gloria would shift from a direct answer when she didn't want to comment. She never lied to him. Just gave him a true answer to a different question! He started to eat the chicken leg and second joint and pickle she handed him on a plate.

She headed out the door. "I put a towel out for you. Just make yourself comfortable and get some rest so you are fresh tomorrow for Gilman's!"

"Sure, Mother Gloria, I will," he said with a smile, which she returned, then left.

Harold finished, rinsed his dish, took some of his things upstairs, used the bathroom, then walked down the stairs to the turn. He looked down to check his footing on the triangular steps. As he stood there he thought what huge changes had happened to him in the last few days.

He was off on his own with a car and a job. If he didn't have to save for college, he could pay rent for a place, maybe not as nice as the little house Peter King was renting, but something. He had left his parents' home without regret. He would miss some friends, but they would soon be heading in their own directions anyway, most of them to college from his advanced section. He knew he would run into them when he was at his parents' or at reunions his high school had. "If we are friends now, we'll always be friends."

He realized he had a lot to learn at Gilman's Hardware, but that would come easily. He remembered Kirke Brown's comment to the young man working for him, that since he learned a lot, he should pay Kirke Brown, not the other way around. He realized that part of the reason it was funny was that there was some unanticipated truth to it.

He thought back to Mike and the accident. He decided to write something down about the event and what Mike said. He still didn't have the whole thing sorted out in his mind. Then from the unsorted part of his mind came the image of Marion, who had impressed him with her assertiveness and the way she handled the bikers and the state cop. She certainly didn't have to lean on a man. But the overwhelming negative thoughts of her attitudes toward colored people pushed the rest aside. Part of him really didn't like her. Another part was more forgiving due to the way she had been raised.

And still from the unsorted area came his feelings about being told by Gloria of his Indian ancestry. He knew of his mother's father's ancestry as English with the name "Eberheart." He always had wanted it to be "Lionheart." He turned and walked upstairs and looked at the blanket, then went downstairs and looked at the other. He still liked the one with the border, and it wasn't worn either. He laughed to himself and realized that his ancestry really didn't determine his views or outlooks. After all, didn't the English have tea every afternoon? He recalled the only times he ever drank tea was when he was buying his car from Mrs. Johnson and later at Kirke Brown's.

He decided he should spend some time writing, organizing his thoughts. He felt he had enough new things to think about and decided to go see what was growing in Gloria's garden.

Chapter 9

> "black Zenith radio": A Transoceanic AM-FM short-wave. You could even hear "Radio Moscow."

10
Starting at Gilman's

Harold walked into Gilman's Hardware about five minutes before seven, his starting time. Mrs. Gilman was there, apparently waiting for him.

"Well let's get going with the first things I have to show you. I had hoped to do the preliminaries before we open, but let's get going.

"Have you ever used a cash register before?"

"Oh yes, I had to ring up everything at Green's, whether snacks or the other things we sold."

"Good. Count the money." Harold hit 'no sale,' counting twenty dollars in change and bills.

"Fine, that is where we start. Every time you get fifty dollars more, when no one is around you put an even fifty under the drawer. When you have a hundred, you give it to me or Gil. Never let anyone see you do this. If someone is on the check list, you can take a check for the amount, like from the boat rental place, but they have to be on the list. You tell others, 'We only take checks from established accounts.' If they want one, they see me. Period. Checks don't count toward the fifty dollars. Do you understand so far?"

"Sure."

"When people bring you things you ring up the amount from the tag, then either take off the tag and put it in the day's page of this book under the counter or write down the number and price if it won't come off. This is so we can reorder. It doesn't matter who bought what except on the register. But don't miss or forget or we might run out. If there isn't a tag or someone took it off, don't guess or take their word for it. Go look if you know where it is or get me or Mr. Gilman to tell you. No exceptions. Understand?"

"Yes ma'am." He remembered an older friend telling him about going in the Army.

"So to start, you will tend the register. If the customers have a lot, or are old or women, offer to carry things out to the car. Then get back in quickly. By the way, Harold, park your car all the way down at the fence so you don't take the close spots."

"When some cute girl comes in, I don't want you wanderin' around the store with her. Your place is right here. Some days get really busy. Go to the bathroom before you start. You get fifteen minutes break for lunch but take it when we aren't too busy. When it is slow we will have you carry stock in and so forth."

"Yes, ma'am." These words, often repeated, became the keys to Harold being assured of a summer job.

11

King of Normandy

Peter King rented the little house. As he and Harold were moving his things in and moving an old sofa to the barn, Peter slipped a bit. Harold had tried to ignore his leg and his cane, but when they put the sofa down for a rest, Harold just asked, "Is your leg okay? How did you hurt it?" Peter sat on the sofa outside of the house.

"Harold, I'm sure you have heard about the landing at Normandy."

"Yes sir, Mr. King. In history, of course, but everybody knows how Ike put together the invasion. The Longest Day. Our teacher introduced that history lesson by asking what month had two 'longest days' in it. We finally got it: June. Were you there? I never met anyone who was."

"Yes. First though, I hear 'Mr. King' enough at school. You are an adult. I would prefer 'Pete.' I was born in 1917. I was working my way through college and didn't get drafted right away. I enlisted in '42 and went through training, then waited, first here, then they started shipping us to England. I got there in late 1943. Then we started training over there. Of course they didn't tell us what we were training for, but we knew it was going to involve going ashore from boats. As one of my buddies said, 'We sure as hell aren't getting ready to capture Iceland!'

"I think a lot of the Brits; sort of hoped we would land at Dunkirk to get revenge in a way. But, we knew the generals would decide and what we thought or wanted really didn't matter. I think they let rumors circulate, hoping the Germans would keep getting different stories if they had any spies around.

"As a corporal wet behind the ears, I knew my squad would land where we were told and follow the sarge and our lieutenant. Into hell as it worked out.

"When morning came, and I could finally see, I was overwhelmed by the number of ships and the size of the force they carried. We had the fortune to land at Omaha Beach. I still don't know what the French call it. We lost about two thousand troops there.

"We were under Colonel Taylor. He was right out there. We started losing guys right away. A couple demolition guys I had been talking to the day before drowned with all their equipment going ashore. Lots died right on the beach. We got off the beach as fast as we could, right into a German machine gun emplacement. Someone showed me a newspaper later quoting what our Colonel said. 'Two kinds of people are staying on this beach, the dead and those who are about to die.' Funny that charging a machine gun was the safest thing to do!

"Well, I made it through the day, off the beach. I will not talk about the fighting. I take no joy in remembering shooting fellow humans, no matter how misdirected they were. I had to shoot to survive.

"The next day we advanced on almost no sleep, but glad to be alive. The guy next to me didn't see a mine. He was killed right away. I was hit in the leg. I knew both bones were bad and I dropped, trying to hold something on it to stop the bleeding. A medic arrived, tied a band near my knee and gave me a needle of morphine right in my stomach. He started sewing up the opening but I don't remember much from then on until I was throwing up on a boat going back to England. Then to an Army hospital."

"In the U.S.?"

"Oh no, I had to stay in England for a while. I wrote a letter to my fiancée telling her not to worry, that we were going to win the war. I told her I had been injured in the leg but had good care in England and I was safe. I wrote her encouraging letters when I could. I did not tell her that to save my life they had to amputate my leg below the knee. The description was too gruesome right then. I knew she would worry that I might get an infection or gangrene or would just worry. In a way I was right.

"They kept us wounded there for months. The only thing that mattered was heading for Berlin. One fellow that came into the hospital had been with Patton. He told me a story that said it all. Patton had told his major in charge of supplies to keep up with his troops and have the necessary amounts of ammunition, guns, parts, everything, delivered on time. When Patton said do it, they did it! There was only one problem. A single lane of track led to the front in that area. There were no sidings near the front. So the major simply directed the French railway people to load the trains one after the other and head east. They did. When the supplies arrived at the front they were unloaded and the cars tipped over into a ravine next to the tracks. Then the next load was brought in and the process repeated. A French railway official saw what was being done with 'his cars.' He raced to Patton and demanded the major be court-martialed. Patton told him the major was following his orders and would the Frenchman prefer they protect 'his cars' and learn to speak German instead of French.

"We were well cared for in England. Getting us home was not a priority. I got fitted with a prosthesis. I learned to walk with a cane. It was hard. At first I felt my leg that wasn't there. Like a ghost. But I got used to it. They developed a lot of new things for artificial limbs as a result of the war. I guess that is good."

"Well you sure do fine. Should you be carrying this sofa, though?"

"I pretty much know what I can do and what I can't. I can lift the weight, but I get a bit off balance carrying in front or behind me. Don't baby me. I'll tell you what I can't do. We can carry this out to the barn in a minute. Harold, you know this is what men are for, moving furniture," he said with a bigger smile than usual.

They carried the sofa out without further rest and put it off to the side with other old things. It might be needed some day.

Pete went back to his new place, Harold to Gloria's house. He wondered if Pete had won any medals but did not plan to ask out of respect for his feelings. Curious as ever, he wondered about the fiancée Pete mentioned. Had they married? He liked Pete.

Chapter 11

> Earl Baney had an auto wrecker's yard in Bellefonte, PA mentioned in Chapter 1. He told the author the above story about Patton. Earl helped tip freight cars during the Battle of the Bulge.
> Colonel George A. Taylor, who led his troops against a German machine gun emplacement and said, according to an Allied Pool news report, "Two kinds of people are staying on this beach, the dead and those who are about to die." More than 2,000 Americans died there.

12

Lisa by the Road

Harold avoided some little bits of junk as he came up the road to Gloria's one damp June afternoon. Then ahead of him he saw a brown '50 Plymouth pulled over. The two left tires appeared flat and a young woman was in front of it looking underneath at the left front tire. He carefully pulled in behind her, avoiding old metal parts that had apparently been dropped on the road, maybe out of a pickup.

He walked up and said, "Can I give you a hand?"

"I don't know what to do. I have one spare and two flats."

"Do you live around here? I could give you a ride home."

"Our farm is about a mile up the hill but I am not going to get in a car with someone I don't know."

"My name's Harold Jenkins. I am staying with Gloria Eberheart, my aunt, and I work at Gilman's."

"I know her, but I never saw you at Gilman's. No thanks."

"I just started for the summer."

"I still don't know you."

"I'm really a nice guy."

"Well, then if you are, drive up the hill and tell my father what happened and he can come down."

"What's your name so I can tell him?"

"I really don't know you. Just describe my car and me."

"How do I know which farm?" Harold was a bit chagrined.

"It is the second lane on the left after you pass Miss Eberheart's. If you are staying at her house, you can find it."

Harold turned, got in his car and drove carefully up the hill. Girls usually were glad to meet him and he was a bit miffed. Passing Gloria's, he found the lane and drove into an old farm similar to Gloria's and neat as a pin. Barn nicely painted. Even the outbuildings. Fences in good order. He parked by the house and heard a tractor coming. He stood and waited.

A big man got off the tractor and came towards him.

"Yes, young man, what can I do for you?"

"Well, sir, do you have a daughter who drives a brown '50 Plymouth?"

Anxious suddenly, the farmer asked, "Is there something the matter with Lisa?"

"She wouldn't give me her name but some fool dropped metal parts on the road about a mile towards the river and she got two flat tires. She's fine. I offered her a ride but she didn't know me. I'm Harold Jenkins, Gloria's nephew."

"Oh, you the one Gil hired for the summer?"

"I'm the one."

"I'm Aaron Burkholder. Thank you very much, young man. I'll go take care of things." He went inside to the kitchen, then came out, got in his pickup and headed down the lane. Harold stood there a minute, alone, then turned around and headed for Gloria's.

That night, he recounted the incident at dinner.

"So you met the Burkholders. They have a nice farm and Lisa is a very bright girl. She finished high school early and goes to Juniata College. I think she even got a scholarship there. She used to come in to the library frequently after school. She's strong willed like me as you found out! She always calls me 'Miss.' They are Church of the Brethren like the college, but from what she has told me, she is a lot more free-thinking than they are. It is a very good school. When she was applying, she told me their motto: 'Veritas liberat' - the truth shall make you free. But I think she takes it a bit differently than in the Bible. She teaches kids at a camp in the summer. I think she has four brothers, all younger.

I remember leaving the library one day and she was driving that brown Plymouth. A couple of guys started kidding her about driving a brown car. She just got a bit huffy with them and said, 'I like my brown car' and drove off. If you are interested, Harold, plan to wait a while. She won't be a pushover even for a cute guy like you."

Harold, somewhat embarrassed, said simply, "I don't think I'm interested."

June 20, 1958

I told Aunt Gloria I wasn't interested in Lisa Burkholder, I guess that's how you spell it, but now here I am up in my room and I keep thinking about her. I guess it is 'cause she is different from the girls I am used to. Most of them would have been glad for a ride in my car. But true, they know me from school and at Ridgeford most people know all about each other for good or bad. I never thought about it before but if I were her father I don't think I would want her getting in the car with some guy she didn't know no matter how nicely he talked! We'll see.

13

Café Society

After dinner Gloria surprised Harold by saying, "Harold, you have been very polite by not inquiring about my life long ago, but I think it will be good for me and good for you to tell you a bit.

"I told you I was sort of wild for those days. From the time I was seventeen I was in love with Joe Schmidt from Annville east of here. He may be the one you heard your parents talking about. We ran into each other at the Pennsylvania State Fair in Harrisburg. Back then it was okay to go to the fair and lots of young people went to see who they might meet. Sort of like they go to Bandstand in Philadelphia and dance on TV now.

"In 1939 in the fall I talked Joe into taking me all the way to New York City. I wanted to see what it was like. I used to listen to jazz on the one station that played it and listened to records at a friend's house. We didn't have a record player. Dad had a pretty good radio with an antenna on it. We used to listen to FDR, who encouraged Dad as he did many others.

"I had heard of a night club in Greenwich Village called Café Society that opened the year before where Billie Holiday sang and we went there. She was great. I had heard that Eleanor Roosevelt and Paul Robeson went there but we didn't see them. Joe didn't know anything about jazz like I did, but he was so in love with me that he probably would have taken me to California to get a basket of oranges.

"Billie Holiday finished a song, I forget what it was. Then it all got quiet like the people knew something was going to happen. We just sat there in the back. We weren't used to such places since it was in New York and there were both colored and white people sitting together in the audience. There were several white women sitting with colored men. Then she started to sing 'Strange Fruit'. I listened intently to every word:

'Southern trees bear a strange fruit...'

"It was about how Negroes were lynched in the South. The song became very famous and was banned in some areas. I have a copy of it somewhere. I'll let you read it, but it is terribly unpleasant."

"Everyone sat silently for a while when she was done, then applauded. We found out she had recently started singing it. I was almost in tears. Joe was shocked. He politely applauded with the others. After a pause, the show went on with something lighter. I realized others knew the song. I had never heard it before but have not forgotten it to this day.

"We didn't talk about it when we left that night. We stayed over with a girlfriend of mine who had gone to Columbia.

"The next day when we were driving back, Joe asked me what I thought about it. I told him it shook me up, but after I thought about it I realized it happened that way and then I told him about my mother being Indian. I told him they just shot my grandfather and a lot of other Indians. They didn't bother to hang them. They just shot them or gave them smallpox. My ancestry didn't bother him in the least. He asked why I hadn't told him before. I told him that some people don't use the term 'half breed' in a very nice way and that my mother just never mentioned her ancestry. He told me about stories from where he came from near Annville about Indians coming down through Swatara G a p and killing some of his ancestors. But that was back before 1750 so he didn't think much about it. Just old stories to him.

"But it turned out that they meant something to his parents. When we talked later about getting married they made it clear to him that they didn't want him marrying me. It amazed me how fear and hate can carry down for generations, but I realized I don't have very good feelings for those who shot my grandfather in 1890. A 'battle' they called it where only lots of Indians were killed. Harold, I know you want to know more, but that is all I can handle right now."

77

Two days later Harold and Gloria were finishing dinner when there was a knock at the door. A tall woman in a plain dress stood there and next to her was Lisa Burkholder. Harold assumed the woman to be her mother. Lisa had something in her hands with a cloth napkin over it. Gloria greeted them.

"Esther, Lisa, come right in! It has been too long since I've seen either of you. We just finished dinner."

"We just stopped by to drop this off to you. We were baking pies and Aaron said we should bring one over to thank your nephew for telling him about Lisa being stuck on the road. It's strawberry-rhubarb. We hope you like it."

Harold smiled widely at the pie. He had tasted strawberry but never tasted strawberry-rhubarb. But Lisa was actually smiling in his direction and that made him sure he would love the pie. For one of the few times in his life he couldn't think of anything to say, so he just smiled, now both at the pie and Lisa.

"Esther, come on in the parlor and sit for a minute. Lisa, thank you. Just put the pie on the counter next to the sink."

As the two left the room Harold gathered his wits and finally spoke. "Aunt Gloria speaks well of you. She says you finished high school early and got into college and work at a camp near here. How do you like Juniata?"

"You sure find things out quickly. It's Harold, right?"

"Yes, Harold."

"Juniata is really nice. A bit strict in some ways, but they have great teachers. I didn't want to go where you had to join a sorority and they don't have them or fraternities either. I think people should all be treated the same. They have interesting traditions like 'mountain day' and various things."

"What's that, a day to climb mountains each year?"

"Sort of. They don't tell you when it's going to be. But each fall, on a beautiful day, all classes are suddenly canceled and everyone goes off to a state park for a day of fun and games. A tug of war, horseshoes, silly stuff like hide and seek, whatever, and a picnic. They have a good theater department. They even do Greek classics like Agamemnon this year. I wasn't in it but I saw it. All School Night is fun too. Each class gets people together to spoof something about the school or the people there."

"How about you Harold? Are you going to college?"

"Oh sure. Franklin and Marshall in Lancaster. I looked at Princeton and Swarthmore, but Princeton doesn't...isn't co-ed and I want a co-ed school. Swarthmore was just too close to home. F and M has a great history and wrestling is important, so I can continue that and I think it helped me get in. It does have fraternities but I don't think I'll get into that. You don't have to. It's about an hour from here, and not too far from home, but far enough."

"I know what you mean!"

Harold and Lisa sat in the kitchen and talked until Esther and Gloria came back from the parlor. They all sat down and tried the pie. Harold found he loved strawberry-rhubarb pie.

Harold had remembered to get a card for his mother. It had flowers on the front and said, "Thank You." Under the "Thank You" inside he added," for always being such a good Mom. Harold." He enclosed a typed letter.

June 22, 1958

Dear Mom,

Well, the job is going fine. I just do it and then go home to Aunt Gloria's or do other stuff. It is just there. But I get plenty of hours and some of the customers are pretty nice and interesting. They talk to me about things like projects they are doing or fish they have caught.

Mrs. Gilman is really the boss. She is fussy and everything has to be done her way. But once you get the hang of it, it all makes sense.

When I first started she reminded me of the boot camp sergeant an older friend once told me about! He got used to the sergeant and I am getting used to her.

Aunt Gloria really surprised me when she happened to say that my grandmother who died before I was born was a Sioux Indian. I guess you never wanted to complicate my life as I grew up by telling me. But I think it is cool. Maybe I could be the next Tonto on TV like Jay Silverheels! Yes, kemo sabe.

My car is running fine. The last work I did on it before school was out took care of everything. I haven't had a problem. Knock on wood.

Met a nice girl named Lisa Burkholder. Sort of what you would call straight-laced. Her car had two flat tires but she wouldn't let me give her a ride up to her farm so I went and got her father. Then another day she and her mom brought a strawberry-rhubarb pie to thank me. She's my age but already has finished one year of college. Real smart.

Hope both of you are well and it doesn't take too long to get this letter to you. I should have written sooner, I know.

Love,
Harold

Chapter 13

> Though the song Strange Fruit, a song about the lynching of black people, was made famous by Billie Holiday, it was written by a Jewish man from New York, Abel Meeropol, who wrote under the name of Lewis Allan. He later adopted the two

sons of "atom bomb spies" Julius and Ethel Rosenberg after their 1953 executions. See the internet for all of the words.

> Also see the internet about Cher's song, "Half Breed" from 1973.

14
Folded Letters

"In a way this is the next part of my story I realize you want to know," Gloria said as she came down from upstairs after dinner another day and handed Harold a browned envelope. Harold took it and read silently.

April 10, 1944

Dear Miss Gloria:

Ma'am, I'm a Medic with His Majesty's 1st Infantry. I am sorry for your loss. I'm sure the officers from the U.S. 36th Engineers contacted you. There was nothing I could do for your Private Joseph Schmidt when we found him. It appears the jeep he was driving was fired on, then turned on to a mine, then over on him. These were in an envelope with your name and address so I am sending them to you. Too many brave lads are gone, but we got to do this thing to the end.

Yours truly,

Cpl. Brian Scott

January 24, 1944

Dear Glory,
Sorry it has been so long. All sorts of security has been in effect since we landed in southern Italy. I think of you every day though and keep your photo always with

me. It is getting worn. Anyway I can send this in a couple of days because the nazis really know where we are! On Jan 22 we totally outflanked them by landing almost unopposed at Anzio way up the coast not far from Rome. Though Mussolini surrendered, the nazis still hold Rome and much of Italy. They didn't know we were coming and we have been busy building roads and landings so more supplies can get in. I am dead tired, but the scuttlebutt is we are about to run for Rome and trap them between us and the guys who hold the south. One guy said that us enlisted guys make the best generals. The brass think too much. We know what ought to be done and what has to be done cause we do it every day. You know how I feel about the nazis. You know how I feel. I get kidded about being named Schmidt and guys have said why don't I change my name to Smith or something. That sets me off on my ~~ these are goddamned nazis who have infected Germany like a disease that is spreading and it is not my way and we damn well have to stamp it out. There is one American Jap guy who knows what I mean. He wanted to go to the Pacific, but they wouldn't let him. His cousin was a mess boy on the Arizona. All he was doing was working on breakfast. We talk a lot when the shelling is heavy. One guy wrote his girl, I love you but if I don't make it, remember me but find someone when the time comes and live your life. That is how I want it if anything happens. Glory I want to be with you in the worst way and don't really want to be here but you know I have to be here. It looks like we'll move out soon.

Goodnight dear Glory,

Joe

January 28, 1944

Dear Glory,

One of us grunts ought to be in charge. The general is so cautious we are just sitting here and the nazis have surrounded us with reinforcements of more than we have. I guess we have 80,000 in this little piece of hell. I bet they have 100,000 and big guns, one especially. We're all digging in as best we can when we could be seeing the sights in Rome. Like I said in the other letter which I will mail with this one when I can, I miss you something awful. Sometimes I fear never seeing you again. We're taking casualties. The nazi bastards even hit our hospital ship. You can't help but see the Red Cross on it. Something I want you to know. I told you about the Japanese guy and there are some colored medics with one of our units and there are two guys from New York, two Mohawks who know steelwork. We are all here. When I get home I'm not going *to let it come around in time like we said about my family. I'm just going to tell them we are getting married and not one word about your mother being Sioux and if they don't like it they don't have to come. You are the one for me and that's all there is to it.*

All my love Dear Glory,

Joe

June 24, 1958

I had wondered why no one told me 'til now I was part Indian but after reading the letter from Joe and hearing about Café Society from Gloria, it begins to make a bit more sense. But I am the same person, aren't I? So why would people treat me any differently if they knew I were part Sioux? I hate questions I don't have a ready answer to.

Joe sure was in love with Aunt Gloria. But still he went off to war and got killed. I hope I never face that decision in my life. I think it is sort of cool how he wouldn't use a capital letter when he writes "nazis."

I think Miss Rose would allow that! I think it is also neat that he kept his name and wouldn't let them take away his good feelings about his German ancestry. His ancestors didn't cause the war or the atrocities. I remember in school when they showed our senior class those movies from the death camps where they killed the Jews. They warned us they would be upsetting. I remember

Margie and Liz heading for the girl's room and Lou told me later that Margie was so upset that she threw up. Liz was quieter for weeks after and seemed to write more in her notebook.

15

Garden and Woods

Harold was home from work when Gloria arrived from the library later than usual. She looked weary and he asked if she were all right.

"Just tired, Harold. We had a meeting with one of the Board's committees, looking over our shoulders to see we don't buy the wrong books. That McCarthy started it. As if we make people become Communists for reading the wrong book!

"But do me a favor. Go out and pick some nice salad makings from the garden. You are just going to get some cheese and bread and salad for dinner, and of course, pie!"

When Harold returned with greens in the splint basket she used for gathering, he said, "Aunt Gloria, when I got here you told me, 'My garden and the woods are my church.' What did you mean by that? I mean I like your garden and I like to walk up the path through the woods to the old fence at the top of the hill, but what did you mean?"

"Have some lemonade and sit down. Let me relax and I'll think about it. How was your day?"

"I really want to hear what you say, but I can wait. I'm getting used to Mrs. Gilman. The formula is easy: You do everything exactly like she wants, like a machine, and everything's fine. Her system does work. I can think of other ways to do stuff, but why bother? I am there to make money. Most people are pretty nice. She doesn't get upset if they initiate the conversation and there isn't a line. She feels I am keeping them happy and that it gives them time to think if there is anything else they need. She did get a bit upset with me today. But then laughed at me as a 'city' boy.

"We were slow by ten and I was unpacking boxes. We had gotten a shipment in and they had sent us a duplication of one box of white enamel ware. She decided it was easier to keep it and call them and argue for an extra discount than to send it back. She got the discount so she told me to set up a display in the window so we might sell some extra. Sounded like a good idea to me and I took out the spring planting things and put them in stock and carefully made a really neat and symmetrical display.

"'Harold, why are you trying to make people laugh at us? Why did you do that?' She almost yelled when she came in from looking at it. I just stood there. I had no idea what she was upset about or what she meant. I just looked at her with a quizzical look on my face. I didn't apologize or say anything.

"'Change it right away!' she said. I replied, 'Mrs. Gilman, I am sorry but I don't know what you are talking about.'

"Then she cracked a little smile. 'You really don't, do you, you city boy! You put the chamber pot right in the middle. I don't think you even know what it is, do you?'

"I looked in the window and said, 'I don't know what most of those white things are for, I just tried to arrange them neatly around that big one you are pointing at. You mean it's like a toilet?'

"As I took it out and rearranged, I asked if there were any others I should take out. She shook her head and went about her work."

Gloria brought over the salad and smiled at him, "Smart city boy; well, you learned something today!"

She sat down and began more of her story. "My mother, whose name was Carol, was raised near a little Episcopal mission at Pine Ridge, South Dakota. She told me stories about her youth. She and her mother weren't close. One person she really liked was an Episcopal Sister named Margaret, who was an Oglala. She worked with the younger people."

Harold looked a bit puzzled and said, "I thought Catholics had 'sisters' but I never heard of Episcopal sisters."

"They aren't very common around here, but they are similar to nuns in lots of ways and I understand most work in some sort of mission.

"After she met and married my father, my mother found it best to attend the Methodist Church where he was raised. I don't think she ever actually joined, but I know she was well thought of at dinners. She was a great cook and didn't mind the work of cleaning up. Like I told you, she just let herself fit in. When she died she was buried as Carol Eberheart and then later Dad's name was added to the stone and he was buried next to her.

"But I never went to church after she became sick. I went to her services of course, but I just had no feeling for it. I couldn't be told that I was to believe something. Once I met a nice looking guy, before Joe, who really got interested in me and very soon invited me to a revival meeting. I said I wasn't very interested in churches but he insisted it was because I had gone to the wrong church and this would be special. He was nice and enthusiastic and I liked him enough to go and see.

"But this loud preacher went on and on and on about how we were all sinners and needed to be saved or perish in hell for eternity and after an hour and a half he almost demanded that we come forward and accept Jesus Christ. Donnie got up and held his hand to me to come and I just sat there. He walked away and hardly spoke another word to me and drove me home and didn't even open the door of his car when he dropped me off. That alone would have been enough to turn me away from his beliefs!

"But I was more thoughtful than that, Harold. I knew one boy's attitude didn't matter in the whole scheme of things, but as a girl, I didn't like it.

"Though my mother was raised with influence from the Episcopal Church and later went to Dad's Methodist church where she was socially involved, she never tried to tell me to believe anything. She talked to me about how I treated people and we talked as I approached teenage years about what was the way to be harmonious - that is the word she used, harmonious - with life and other people. Her test was not what one believed or said they believed, but how they made others feel.

"Gardening is like that in a lot of ways. You can't plant broccoli in January, even in a thaw. Corn needs time to grow and sun. But has to be in early enough to get its growing season in, but not so soon it freezes, but it can't go in too late because September comes and it won't properly mature if it is planted too late. If we all shot does when they were carrying fawns, we would drastically cut the size of the herds and cut our meat supplies. Some people think it strange that I hunt, but I see no difference between eating beef or pork or venison, and I like venison.

"Ever notice that some trees can't grow in the shadow of other trees? Or that rabbits don't like to go in a garden with marigolds around it?"

"I thought you just liked to see the different bright colors of their flowers. They really keep rabbits away?"

"Probably not one hundred percent, but they help a lot. Hanging out some old smelly socks helps keep deer away since they get the human scent. So in my garden and woods, I see lots of cases of the harmony my mother felt so important. And I have read a lot about the sky and the stars and beyond. Did you ever think about how big this universe is? 'What is man that Thou art mindful of him,' asks one of the psalmists of Biblical times. Harold, did you ever think how insignificant we are? They say at burials, 'dust into dust.' Many Indians express that the earth does not belong to us, but that we belong to the earth.

"I touch the earth each time I am in my garden and it touches me. I have seen pictures of the great cathedrals of Europe and they are a testament to wonderful craftsmen and designers, but are their arches any more glorious than the canopy of the oaks up the slope to the west?

"Over the years I have read a lot from different parts of the world. In India thousands of years ago someone wrote,

'Yesterday is but a dream, tomorrow, is only a vision, but today, well lived, makes all our yesterdays dreams of happiness and all our tomorrows visions of hope.' So without a lot of people telling me how, I try to live well today. I allow them to live their ways. My garden and my woods surround me and if I look closely, I see what they have to teach me about life and how to act in this world. I don't fear any hell like that preacher used to make people act the way he wanted. I don't ask any reward. Isn't doing the right thing, at least to the best of my ability, enough reward in itself?

"But the people in India who could see this truth got so bogged down in all sorts of gods like Shiva and castes that made one group higher than another. Then recently when Gandhi and others led them to independence they got to killing Muslims and Muslims killed Hindus and Gandhi was killed and fighting broke out and they divided the area into India and Pakistan. Is this what religion is about?"

She paused, then finished. "I better get dinner. I'm starting to sound like a preacher!"

The next morning, Saturday, Harold was stocking the store.

"Excuse me, but I need a pack of ten-inch 32-tooth hacksaw blades." Lisa smiled as Harold turned at her voice behind him.

"Lisa!" Harold turned and stood looking at her, his hands holding boxes of nuts and bolts he was about to put in their containers. "I didn't hear you come in. Aren't you working today? I mean I think Aunt Gloria said you worked Saturdays on your farm most weekends." He didn't want to appear too anxious or too interested, but his eyes gave him away.

"You were so intent on what you were doing that I thought of just saying, 'Boo,' but I thought you might drop things all over the floor. My father is making something and needs some blades. And yes, I usually work today but we shifted around some. How late do you work?"

He put the boxes down. She was wearing jeans and a loose fitting plaid shirt and sneakers. Her hair pulled back with a couple of barrettes. No makeup, no pretense. Helping her father that day.

"I get off at four. You helping your father?

"For a while. Listen, there is a pizza place down in Lemoyne and some group, I don't know their name, sort of like the Kingston Trio, is going to be there tonight. I wondered if you would like to go. A couple of friends from school are going and I thought it would be fun."

"Sure, I would love to. What time should I pick you up?"

"Well, Harold, I asked you and the understanding I have with my parent is if I drive my car somewhere with a friend or friends, I don't have to ask permission. I would have to ask to have you pick me up. So I'll pick you up about seven at Gloria's, if that's okay."

Harold had once been asked to a Sadie Hawkins dance but never asked out with the girl driving before. So he gathered up his courage and said the only thing he could think of.

"Sure. That sounds cool to me. Come on down here and I'll get the blades for your father.

"These what you need?" He handed her the cellophane-wrapped pack of six.

With a smile she said, "You are the hardware expert! I'm sure these are what he wants."

They went to the counter and she paid for them and left with hardly any words, just her bright smile again. Harold finally remembered what he had been doing and got back to stocking nuts and bolts.

Harold was all ready and sitting in the kitchen at seven when Lisa pulled in the drive. Aunt Gloria had thought it was fine that Lisa should drive. She told Harold to just relax and enjoy her company and not to talk so much that he bothered her driving. He said he would try to remember and headed out the door, waving as Lisa turned her brown Plymouth around. He did like his silver Chevy better, but he would keep that to himself!

By the time they got down to Routes 11 and 15 headed south, Harold had relaxed. She knew how to drive. "What kind of a camp do you work at, Lisa?"

"It's for crippled children. Usually they have polio but some have cerebral palsy, some muscular dystrophy, multiple sclerosis and so forth. It was really hard at first, but once you get to know them as kids and individuals, you see their ups and downs. Some days a kid will have more trouble talking or wheeling his chair, but then another day is better. I can't believe how happy most are, despite their problems. Of course we get the kids who can and want to go to camp. I know there are lots who never leave their bedrooms where they live. Did you ever wonder if some people are born happy and stay that way no matter what happens to them? Some of these kids are that way and can't walk or use their arms very well or talk well, but still even make jokes when you can understand them."

"I think you are right. At Ridgeford we saw some movies on the Holocaust and it upset lots of people. But I got to know an old lady who lived a couple of blocks from the snack bar where I worked. She would come in on a hot day for lemonade or something. Though she never spent much, she always left me a tip. We got talking about history and the war and she told me how glad she had been when the soldiers got to Auschwitz. She just put all the evil behind her once she was free and wrote her cousin who was a cantor in Bala Cynwyd near Philadelphia. She told me his family had lived in the Philadelphia area since the eighteenth century. He replied as soon as he heard from her and made all the arrangements and brought her here. Then he bought a three apartment building and gave her one apartment and rented the other two. He told her it was in the deed that she could live there for the rest of her life, rent free. She said this was a 'mitzvah' to him but I never quite understood that. She got a job in a dress shop and learned good English and became a citizen when she was fifty-five. I never saw her but she had a smile and said a good word about someone. And she had lost her husband and three children to the gas chamber."

"That is exactly what I am talking about. Doesn't she make you feel good when you see her? You are lucky to have met her, Harold."

"I'm glad *we* got to meet. I guess I should tell you I was a bit miffed when I offered you a ride that day, but you were right. You didn't know who I was. I am sure glad you and your mom brought over that strawberry-rhubarb pie..."

Lisa just turned to him, smiled, and looked to the road. That was fine with Harold. They continued to Lemoyne. He thought of how she differed from Marion who got right in.

Sunday afternoon when Harold came home from work, Aunt Gloria looked at him with a slightly quizzical look as if to say "How was last night?" Harold did not miss the look.

"I see that look, Aunt Gloria. The pizza was real good. The group turned out to be just okay, but I had a real good time with Lisa and her friends. I told them about just finding out that my grandmother was an Indian and they didn't think it was a big deal or anything. Neither did Lisa. One guy, Eric, goes to Juniata and he brought his girlfriend Beth, and Lisa's roommate, Clara, brought her boyfriend David, so I didn't mind at all being paired with Lisa. And it wasn't an accident. She is really smart and doesn't have much happen by accident. It was the way she wanted it. We sat where people were eating and talked and talked and didn't pay much attention to the show. They just didn't make it. Lisa and I left at a reasonable time since we both had to work today."

Harold left out that it took him quite a while to get to sleep. He and Lisa had agreed to talk again "in a couple of days."

Chapter 15

> "Yesterday is but a dream.." From the Upanishads in Sanskrit.

16
Time to Say Goodbye

June 29, 1958

I don't know if I am older than Lisa is or not. In some ways she seems older, but in a much nicer way than Marion.

Marion was hard and not really conscious of her life. She let things limit her outlook. Sort of tunnel vision. But Lisa thinks about everything or has already thought about it. Actually that is the only thing I find a bit difficult about her. It is a little bit like dancing with a girl who tries to lead. You go to dancing class and line up on opposite sides of the room and choose partners and the lady in charge tells you what to do. She teaches you that the men, or "boys" as she called us, are supposed to take the initiative and the "girls" should be aware of our signals and follow effortlessly. Lisa just goes along, with a pretty good idea of where she is going, and it feels like you can go too, or not. But I really like going along. She is such a nice person and she can talk about anything without putting you down. Like at the pizza place, the group wasn't very good, but she just took it in stride and said something like, "Well, with such nice people we didn't need anything more than background music." And then that smile of hers. Makes me happy to do things a bit differently!

"Harold, I am going to let you read a letter. I care about you and I want to share it with you. Don't be shocked. I just wrote what I wanted to, and had to, about eleven years ago. It was my way of finally accepting that Joe was gone. I don't want to talk about it. I am going out to the garden to work. Don't ask me anything. But if I can tell you about your ancestry, I can tell you about me and Joe. You will see the connection. He was a wonderful man."

Gloria handed Harold a multi-page folded letter that had been typed on her old typewriter. She went out the door to the garden. Harold sat down and read:

February 14, 1947

Dear Joe,

I just have to write this to you. Yes, I know you are gone, three years now and a bit more. And Dad is gone, but that was much easier. He was older and sick and I could, and had to, deal with that and Mom had been gone over ten years so it was okay, but it is still not okay that you are gone. It will never be okay.

I got your two letters from a nice medic who mailed them for you. He didn't have to. Your parents never wrote or stopped by. If it weren't for him I would not have known. I guess I would have gone to your parents, knowing, but having to ask. I don't understand why they can't deal with my Indian ancestry because of a raid in the 1700's. That is just who they are. My sister has never told her son Harold about our mother. But he is only about seven. Remember how happy I was when I saw him that first time? I still thank you for driving me all the way to Philly after Harold was born. If no one tells him about my mother I will when he is old enough. I just have to write this all down, so I can let go.

A friend of mine told me she felt better after she lost her father, a major, by writing him a letter. He was flying an airplane in the Pacific. They never found him but his buddies saw him go down. I read that millions of Jews and maybe fifteen million Russians are dead, to say nothing of you and the other Americans and all the other people in Europe and the Pacific. What a word. Pacific. Peaceful. Why Joe, why do we humans have to do this to ourselves???? Can't we learn?

I guess I am sorry for all those other people but Joe, I am sorry for you and me. Whatever my life holds, I will always love you. I am so glad for those two letters the medic sent for you.

You once told me, "Glory, I'm not a handsome movie star: I just love you so much I feel like one." You always made me feel special. I told you one time that I wasn't any Marlene Dietrich either. I think we were looking at an old Screenbook magazine I found somewhere and she was on the cover. You just turned to me and kissed me so gently, despite being a lot bigger than me.

And I remember when you and I had been working outside helping Dad with something and he went down to Enola to his job and you came in. You were hot and I gave you some lemonade. You always liked it with too much sugar in it!

You would say it had to be as sweet as me.

And you kissed me and I liked your sweaty man smell and I started to tingle all over and pulled you over on the couch and started to touch you and tell you how much I loved your arms and strong legs and everything. Then I pushed you off in fun and lay down and told you to come back. And you sat on the floor next to me and we talked a little and I took your hand and put it under my shirt and told you to touch me. I think I surprised you but you kissed me and touched me and you were so gentle. I remember later asking how a great big guy could be so gentle. And you told me that you had learned to be careful like for helping a newborn calf and I was as soft as they were. I laughed at you for that, sort of saying I was like a calf, but you could see the love in my eyes. Saying I was like a calf!

I will always remember your gentleness, then and every time we touched. You told me you had never touched another girl and I believe you. Still to this day I am amazed at your tenderness. And when I said I wanted you in me that first time you said we had to wait because you said you should not get me pregnant but next time we could -- you would make sure nothing would happen. And then you softly kissed me again. I started to feel all sorts of things I never felt before. And then later after I had calmed down, I said what about you and you said I am happy and next time it will be safe for you. And you kept your word and it was even better when you lay beside me but I always liked that you thought of me first and took so much time.

And when I said I'm not very big and not so pretty you told me that a I was perfect for you and that was all that mattered.

I remember another time I told you an older girlfriend said that guys just want to have their fun and leave. But you said Glory I love you. I love to see you feel wonderful. Us guys are simple creatures, it's easy to make a man feel good. But for me to really be happy I want to spend time pleasuring you and you will know I care about you and do things you want.

You were always so natural, not just when you were close to me, but like when we went up to New York because I wanted to hear jazz and you just talked to people who were different like they were some new neighbor. Even those two guys hand in hand, just said, if that's what they want. Me, I prefer you!

Part of me wanted to hold onto you or make you be like that guy I knew down at the Quaker meeting near Wellsville who was doing service in a hospital. Or Aaron Burkholder's brother, but I knew you had to go. You knew so deep inside of you how wrong it was, what the Nazis were. Sorry Joe, I know you write nazi with no capital. You wouldn't even give them that.

And I remember when we went to that dance down at Dillsburg. That big-busted blonde girl sure took to you. Whenever they changed partners, she tried to be near enough to get you. I started feeling sorry for her. You made it so clear you were spoken for.

I only remember getting mad at you once when you didn't talk to me the same way and sort of acted strange and then I found out your time to go in the Army had come and you couldn't bear to tell me. And then the day before you had to leave, I made you lie down and made you, yes, I had to make you just lie there and let me do everything I wanted, to and for you. I think you were a little embarrassed at first and maybe I was too but I loved you so and wanted you to remember who to come home to and that there wasn't a better place anywhere, not even France, if you got there. I never told you I had found a couple of books in an old shop and read them.

And I know you would have come home to me and we would have had a family, maybe too many kids, if we weren't careful. But you are gone and I am here and today is Valentine's Day and I remember the little box of candy you gave me the first Valentine's after we met, how you made me eat all but the one piece I insisted you eat and I remember your kiss and your gentle touch and I will never forget you my very, very dear Joe. Now you can see my tears on the page and I can't see to type anymore and it is time to say goodbye to you, dear Joe.

Your Glory forever,
Gloria

Harold just sat there, shocked and fascinated at the same time. This was so real and fit in with the rest of the story he had been told. He was a little embarrassed to read it but like

Gloria said, if she could tell him about their ancestry, why not tell him about Joe?

He sat and thought for a while and then he slowly reread it. He stopped at the mention of himself at seven and when he was born and began to see more connection between the letter and her telling him of his Oglala ancestry.

He had heard that millions of Jews were killed but had not known that fifteen million people in the Soviet Union were dead. No wonder they are worried about being attacked from the West. He decided he would have to read more about that. That many dead?

What Aunt Gloria said Joe was like was sure not like the way some guys talked. Get some as quick as you can before she changes her mind was what they seemed to think. He was glad to read what had made Aunt Gloria so happy but still he was a bit embarrassed to read it. Before she went out to the garden she said "Joe was a wonderful man." He realized she was showing him what she considered a good model for himself.

He wondered, if Joe hadn't been killed, what things would have been like for him and Gloria. They would probably live there, have kids, Joe would probably have a good job. What would they be like? Would Aunt Gloria have read so much? What makes people come out the way they do? He thought of the two weavings and considered how the events of life weave together to make us what we are. Do they make us what we are, or is it how we react to this or that, that makes us what we are? He found, for now, that the thoughts generated by the letter gave him more questions than answers. "Interesting consequence of my being so inquisitive," he thought.

Harold walked outside, saw Peter's Pontiac wagon and walked over to it.

17

Of Cars and Bikes: Know When to Fold

"It's my toy, Harold!" Peter said as he walked over to where Harold was looking at his car.

"Is this the one that has the triple two barrel carbs I read about in Hot Rod?"

"No, I thought about that model but this has the four barrel. It's a '57 Chieftain Safari. I thought there just might be too much adjustment needed with trips, but this runs really well and I don't have to worry about it. It's a two-speed Hydramatic, but you can hold it in low then shift it manually like a stick. It is easier on my leg. Ever hear about the guy who nicknamed his teenager 'Hydramatic?' Because he was shiftless."

"That joke is awful, Pete! But the car sure is nice!"

"I live pretty simply and in administration with a masters, I get paid enough. Having the wagon is nice if I want to take things and head off camping. A friend has a place up near Eagle's Mere about three hours north that I like to visit. Trout in the spring and bass in the summer. I never had a hot rod like you have when I was young. It was the Depression and kids just didn't have cars and the family car was pretty old. So I finally got a 'cool' car that I couldn't have back then. Tell me about yours, Harold."

Harold told him about Mrs. Johnson and finding the wrecked Corvette and all the hours and money he'd put into it. "I don't race it, and even if I did, I sure wouldn't run against that big Pontiac V-8!" This was said in a totally complimentary manner, which Peter understood without further explanation.

Harold shifted to another question as Peter sat down on a chair between his car and the little house.

"I guess you and the fiancée you told me about never got married?"

"No, we never did. Tell me something, Harold. If you don't have a girlfriend at the beginning of a school year and you walk into a new class, what is the first thing that gets your interest about a girl?"

"Oh, that's easy. I just sort of look around and see if anyone looks good to me, and then I see if I can catch her eye. But don't get me wrong, I'm very interested in someone right now so I am not looking."

"I'll bet it's that girl you told Gloria you didn't think you were interested in," said Peter with a big smile.

"I just said that, but things have changed a lot since then."

"Yes, I noticed she picked you up the other night. Pretty good deal, Harold. Nice girl and she drives you." Peter was having a bit of fun with him.

"Well that had to do with who we were going to meet and her agreements with her parents, but it worked fine. But back to your question; I guess it is who catches my eye, at least for starters."

"And that is pretty much how my fiancée and I got involved. I was a decent looking academic guy who played tennis fairly well. She was a couple of years younger and I saw her sitting with a girl I played mixed doubles with at a club I went to. She caught my eye just like you said. I arranged for my mixed doubles partner, who was going with a friend of mine, to introduce us. And things went from there. People said what a good looking couple we were. And it turned out we played tennis pretty well together. She was about 5'5" and played a good net game. I could run in the backcourt and anticipate, and had a strong backhand."

"We came from similar backgrounds, and had similar interests and she danced well, as I did. She was a junior in college and I was in grad school and things just seemed to work. We got engaged her senior year and then the war came along and I went into the Army. Almost all my friends did. She really didn't want to work and she got involved with the Red Cross with the support of her parents."

"That sounds like a good thing to do. My Mom never really wanted to work. Did she meet someone else?"

"Well she did about a year after the war was over and got married and has two kids, and all things considered, it was probably for the best for both of us."

"I don't get it. Who broke things off, you?"

"No, as I told you I got wounded and ended up in a hospital in Devonshire in England and they amputated my leg below the knee. I told her I was wounded and getting good care. I wanted her to see me walk off the boat, even with the cane. She was there waving with lots of others and grabbed me and kissed me and we took a cab to the hotel where she was staying and up to her room. She said she wasn't waiting anymore and started to undress. I did too and when I took my pants off she saw I had a prosthesis and lost it. She said I should have told her I wasn't whole. She cried and got dressed and said she was really upset and had to be alone. I got dressed and left and went home to my parents and called her the next day. Her mother said she didn't feel well. Two days later I got a letter from her enclosing her engagement ring and just saying she wished I had told her."

"But if she wanted to marry you and go to bed with you I don't see why it mattered about your leg."

"I thought about that for years, Harold, but I realized to a large degree we were objects to each other. I was attracted to her by looks. Sure, if she had talked like a walrus, I probably wouldn't have stayed interested, but everything fit. But I wasn't a perfect fit anymore; I wasn't 'whole.'"

"But it shouldn't matter. You are the same person who went away."

"No, I wasn't the same person who went away. Besides the leg, I went ashore at Omaha Beach and saw so much. I trained to kill and killed. I have friends who were there who just don't talk about it. She never saw that difference. I didn't see it for a while. But since she couldn't deal with the missing leg, the reason I say it is probably for the best for both of us, is that she never saw the deeper changes."

"How are you and Aunt Gloria getting along?"

"Fine. She has read so much and when we have time, we can talk about anything and I can't imagine a better landlord. She's a fine person. Why do you ask?"

"I think you two have a lot in common. The war really interfered with both your lives. She lost Joe Schmidt at Anzio Beach in Italy. From what I know, he was a really good guy. I am sure they would have been married if he had come back."

"When I told her about my leg she said just to tell her if I had a problem and needed anything and then said only,

'I lost a lot in the war, too.'"

Peter got up and he and Harold walked to the car. Peter opened the hood and showed Harold the very big and clean engine. He obviously took good care of the car, his "toy," and even cleaned the engine compartment from time to time.

At work the next day, Harold listened intently to two firemen. After the accident scene he had witnessed where he helped Mike, he realized firemen saw things most people don't. No one else was in the store. He was supposed to be attentive to customers so he just stood and listened. It had been a summer of lessons and this seemed like one more. They were discussing a woman who had been found dead a week ago, after she had ridden her bike off the road trying to get control rather than "bailing out." She had hit a tree at about 30 miles per hour and was dead when found.

"Were you with the company when we had one like it about ten years ago?"

"No, I joined eight years ago when we moved here."

"Well that time it was a guy on a little motorbike, a Zundapp I think. They are only meant for level places like the shore. I think they use them in Bermuda. He was trying to ride it like a big Indian or something. He got going too fast coming down a hill toward the river and the coroner said later that he had burned off his brakes. Apparently he tried to ride it out with no brakes and hit a curve with gravel on it and went over the edge. We had to climb down about sixty feet to get him. The only reason anyone found him is some guys were hiking and saw the slide marks and checked them out."

"This one had been dead a day. Riding a bike too fast for her brakes. Same type of thing. Tried to ride it out and went off a drop. Dead on impact, poor girl."

"Those are the risks I guess. What can you do about it?"

"That's my point. Both of them could have survived if they thought right even after their initial screw-up. Think about it. Which do you take? Dead? Or a bunch of brush burns, maybe a broken bone or even worse, but alive? You got to know when you are out of control and bail out. In both cases, they could have turned into the bank or tipped to the inside. Either way they would have a much better chance of being alive. Do you play poker?"

"Yeah, not much though."

"Then you've heard, 'Know when to fold.' It is the same thing. But the problem is from the time we are little kids, we hear Mom saying, 'Now be careful, don't get hurt!' And kids catch hell when they come home with something ripped or scrapes."

Harold's mind flashed back to going home after his tussle with Martin on the playground.

"Nobody ever says, 'you did a good job not getting hurt worse.' The only time I ever heard something like that was years ago when our field truck was coming back from getting some service work. The driver had to go about two feet off the road on the right and scraped up the fenders and running board because some idiot driving a gasoline truck had come too fast around the comer. He made the choice to hit the side rather than hit the tanker. We had a real smart Chief. Publicly commended the driver so none of the guys could give him any shit without directly going against the Chief. He got the name of the tanker business and they made a very nice 'donation' to the fire company!"

"So you're saying we ought to teach kids that sometimes you got to take the immediate hurt to avoid something worse."

"You got it, but I don't know how. I've talked to my kids, but for now, we just do what we can when we get a call."

The older fireman put the bolts he had selected down on the counter for Harold to add up. The other headed into the garden section.

18

"In a couple of days"

On the drive back from Lemoyne, they had agreed they would talk in a couple of days but they hadn't been more specific. Harold thought about it at work and decided a couple of things. If he didn't want Lisa to take the initiative all the time, he simply would have to. Second, he still was not used to a girl driving, but realized it was nice since she was a good driver and he could sit there and look at her, which he couldn't do when he was driving. He did know that he never wanted a brown car!

It was Tuesday evening. Since he had finished the things Aunt Gloria had asked him to do when she was at work, and "a couple of days" had passed, he decided just to stop in at her family's farm after she had time to get home from work and finish with dinner. He decided if he saw her father first, he would try to say he respected their agreement about who she drove with and ask permission to take her out sometime.

Thinking about this, he glanced at the table and saw a magazine-size package with his name and Gloria's address in his mother's handwriting. He opened it quickly and found materials from Franklin and Marshall and, in particular, information from the "Reading American Literature for Writing" course he planned to take. There was a copy of Thornton Wilder's *Our Town*. A letter indicated that he was to finish reading it by the time he got to school and to write something brief about the topic "realizing life" during the summer. Keeping his eye on the clock from time to time, he read some, cleaned up, and at about seven, headed up the hill for the short drive to the Burkholders.

He pulled in the drive and saw Lisa sitting on the side porch talking intently with her mother. As soon as she heard his car, she looked his way, turned back to her mother and said something as Harold parked. He got out of the car. As he approached them, Lisa said, loud enough for him to hear clearly, "Mother, here's Harold. We planned to go for a little drive. You don't have a problem with me riding with him, do you? We won't be late at all; we both have to work tomorrow."

Her mother replied a bit coolly as Harold walked over, "No, Harold is fine. Hello, Harold. I didn't know you were coming."

"We planned to talk some more after our nice evening in Lemoyne." Harold replied carefully, sensing something of an undercurrent.

Lisa said to her mother, "You and I got talking so much, I just never mentioned expecting him." Then, "Let's go Harold. We have to be back by ten." Lisa got in without waiting for him to open the door. Harold waved to Mrs. Burkholder as he headed out the drive.

Lisa's smile was a bit different from what he was used to as she said, "Your timing certainly was good. Thanks!"

"We planned to 'talk in a couple of days.' What's up?"

"Let me relax a minute and be glad you arrived. There's an ice cream place a little bit south. I'll buy you a cone and we can sit on their porch and talk."

Harold had no problem with the idea and headed down the hill, then turned right on the main road.

They pulled in and parked, got vanilla cones and sat on the porch overlooking the road. Harold looked at the road quietly, but expectantly, waiting for Lisa.

"Mother and I don't always see eye to eye. I know, most girls and their mothers don't, but our differences are more philosophical. We don't fight about keeping my room clean or helping with dishes and stuff like that. Simple. I like my room in order and I eat and live there so I do my fair share around the kitchen and farm. My brothers are pretty good too. But when we get going, on ideas and what is happening in the world and philosophical and religious ideas, well, we really get going. Do you know what I mean?"

"Sure, Lisa, I avoid dealing with my mother. She is sort of resigned to the fact that I won't go to church with her and when she says anything, I avoid a fight by having something to do or somewhere to go, like tonight; you were glad to go somewhere."

She turned to him very seriously. "Yes, I was glad to have somewhere to go, but just so it is clear, even if we weren't having a bit of a discussion, I was very glad to see you drive in."

Harold was so pleased with her directness. He blushed.

"Thanks, Lisa. What was going on, if it is okay to ask?"

"She feels my soul is in danger because I don't keep to 'our traditional ways' of belief. Brethren aren't anywhere near as strict as the Amish or Old Order Mennonites, but men usually wear beards and women wear simple dresses and cover their heads appropriately and believe in a Father God, Jesus the Son, type of theology that tells us how to live, which is just the way our parents lived, exactly as they read the Bible. They are good and honest people, like not fighting wars and so forth. But so restrictive and dogmatic. We got going on the duty of a woman to be a good wife and to raise children. I said I didn't know when I would get married and that I was not sure about having any children. Bang, 'Be ye fruitful and multiply!' Then she says, 'Any nice young man, like your new friend, Harold, surely wants children.' That was like a cue for you! Thanks for showing up."

Harold thought about what Gloria had said to him about his expectations that young women would marry and have kids. Intellectually, he felt women should do what they wanted.

"Before I picked you up, I was thinking that we said we would talk in a couple of days, so after dinner I read some, then came to see you. And I don't want any kids, at least for quite a while!" He liked the smile that came his way.

"Tell me, Harold, don't you think that things are right or wrong, not because the Bible, says so, or any book for that matter, but just cause they are. You shouldn't kill people. You shouldn't steal and so on."

"That's about how I feel but recently I have thought a lot about wars and the people that have to fight them. Aunt Gloria showed me a letter that mentioned that your uncle was a conscientious objector and I think worked in a hospital during the war. The man she was in love with was killed at Anzio, Italy in 1944 and Peter King, who I think she is interested in, was wounded at Normandy. I know he fought to stay alive, but he doesn't talk about it. I sure never want to be in the position they were in and have to decide. If someone started to attack you, I would grab him. I wrestled in high school, and I'd do what I had to protect you. But I wouldn't want to kill anyone."

"Thanks Harold. They really face guys with tough decisions. Ever think about what it would be like if women fought right alongside of men? I think even though we are smaller and not so strong, we can be tough if forced to be. Ever read about the French Resistance or about the Jews fighting back against the Nazis in the Warsaw Ghetto? I am glad I wasn't there. Part of me is so strong against killing but another part feels so strongly I would be shooting a gun or throwing a firebomb like those women did right with the men. And what happened to them if they were caught?"

"I'd have a hard time seeing you doing that. We studied what happened and saw movies of the death camps. I read that someone asked Gandhi why the Jews had been killed since they were non-violent. He startled the questioner by saying they weren't. They were passive. They cooperated with the Nazis by getting on the trains and leaving their homes and doing what they were told. He said if they had resisted the wrong and refused to leave their homes, it would have forced the good Germans to see them shot in the streets in front of their own eyes. He said that maybe forty or fifty thousand might have died but he believed a revolution would have occurred because although the German people might accept 'relocation' they would have been appalled to see families they knew murdered in front of them in their own towns. He was also pretty clear that it was better to use force to resist injustice than to cooperate

112

with it. Then someone murdered him. Let's get on a more pleasant topic."

"Hey, not so fast. Do you think you could find me the information about Gandhi for a paper this fall? I think we have a lot to learn from him."

"Sure, and I will try to treat you equally, but pardon me if I keep thinking you are a pretty cool girl." He received that nice smile.

Harold heard the typical rumble of a Harley Davidson motorcycle as it slowed and pulled in. Two figures in black got off and walked up the steps. "Thought that was your car, Har. This is Billy, my boyfriend from up in Williamsport. We're headed up there now."

Harold stood up to his full height and shook hands. Lisa remained seated. Harold was very surprised to see Marion, especially at this inopportune moment.

"Figured if you were here, the food was fine. Who's your friend?"

"Marion, this is Lisa. She lives near here."

Lisa remained seated and held out her hand. "Pleased to meet you, Marion. We were just finishing our cones."

"Yeah, we got to get some food. Good to see you Har. Thanks again for that ride."

Harold took Lisa's cue gladly and pulled her chair back and they left. Once in the car she smiled and said, "She really doesn't seem your type, Harold."

Harold headed south and pulled off at a park outlook by the river and stopped. "You are so right. I gave her a ride from Harrisburg to her grand mom's in Philadelphia fairly near home." He told Lisa a short version of the Turnpike Girl story. Then he commented, "I think she just lives in her world and goes along but really doesn't think about things. Like about her father who was just let out of the Army and then left her and her mother and went to San Francisco. And what she says about colored people and how her mother and grandmother brought her up to think that way. I have to think about everything. You're right, she isn't my type. I'm much more attracted to a girl that thinks about things."

Lisa moved over next to him, kissed him on the cheek, and said with that great smile, "Thank you, Harold!"

Harold blushed, then gently put his arm around her and they watched the evening sunlight play on the river and the trees on the opposite shore as the sun set. They talked and were quiet and talked some more. Just the enjoyment of two humans as company for each other, sharing ideas without fear of not being understood.

A little after nine, they left in plenty of time and drove up the road where they first met.

"Do Brethren believe in returning what has been given to them?"

"Yes, in various ways. What do you mean?" Lisa replied as Harold slowed to a stop where she had the two flat tires.

He turned and kissed her very gently on the lips. "Just figured I should give that back before we got to your house!" He started up. He couldn't see her in the dark, but when he got out and walked her to the house she was smiling. Her father was on the porch.

"Glad to see you young people home at a reasonable hour, Harold."

"Yes sir, Mr. Burkholder. I have to work and I am really glad Lisa works too and understands."

Lisa kissed her father and went in with a little "Good night, Harold."

"I expect I'll see you again." Mr. Burkholder held out his hand and they shook.

"Thank you; I hope so, sir," said Harold as he turned for his car, trying not to smile too much.

July 1, 1958

Aunt Gloria wasn't in the house when I got home. Such a nice night. I know I need to get some sleep but I think it will be a good thing if I write some. I still can't believe I told Aunt Gloria "don't think I'm interested." Damn, was I shortsighted.

I guess I was so used to cute little girls just taking my arm or dancing with me and hanging on every word I said. She takes more thinking but she is one neat girl!

Wonder what goes on for Fourth of July out here? It is this Friday and I think we are closed. Better check tomorrow. I remember Pierre, the French exchange student, really quick witted. We told him all about the Fourth of July fireworks and parades then asked him, "Do the French have a Fourth of July?" He answered real quickly and proudly, "No, we have Bastille Day!" Then someone said "Quesque-'ce que vous appelez le jour apres le troisieme juillet?" We finally got him with that.

Another thing I just realized. Lisa is about the only girl not to make a big deal over my Chevy. I can live with that. I am sure she likes riding in it better than some old clunker.

I think I'll read some more of Our Town, then turn in. Nice evening. Guess Aunt Gloria is still out in the garden.

Harold made sure to get to work by five of seven on July second, and at the first opportunity asked Mr. Gilman about the schedule for the Fourth of July. As he did, Mrs. Gilman came over and replied to his question.

"Be here at your usual seven a.m., but we have to close at eleven so you get paid for four hours. It would be a normal work day except the parade comes by here about noon and then everything is messed up the rest of the day even though some people want to buy things, others will have used all our parking lot to watch the parade. So you just have fewer hours this week." She went to her work. Mr. Gilman had nothing to add.

As he worked that morning he was glad to have the time off. He knew some people got a paid holiday when it fell on a weekday, but he had not really expected that to be true here. He just smiled to himself and was amused at the thought that a Fourth of July parade was a detriment. He hoped Lisa had off.

Right after work he wrote his cousin the letter he had been putting off, then put it in the box by the road.

July 2, 1958

Dear Couley,
    Well my favorite little cousin, it is about time I wrote to you to tell you what is going on with me and see how you are doing. I went to visit Aunt Gloria right after graduation and ended up getting a job north of Harrisburg along the Susquehanna, so I can put this in a bottle if I can't find a stamp and send it down the river to you along the Chesapeake!
    I met a girl who was nice enough but was really prejudiced against colored people and I thought of the story you told me about getting ice cream cones. I was proud thinking of you. I happened to see her again while I was getting vanilla cones with a really nice girl who lives up the hill from Aunt Gloria. He name is Lisa and she is really smart like you

are. She skipped a year in high school and has already finished a year of college. So I realized I had to write you.

I am working in a place called Gilman's Hardware and I make enough money to save a good bit for the fall for college. Mrs. Gilman, who is really the boss, is pretty fussy but as long as you do things the way she wants, it isn't bad.

Aunt Gloria is fine. She rented her little house to a guy named Peter King. He walks with a cane and a part of his leg is artificial. He got wounded in World War II at the big invasion at Normandy Beach. He does real well and won't talk about the fighting part. He is the new assistant superintendent of schools for this area. I think he and Aunt Gloria are interested in each other. She told me about a great guy named Joe Schmidt who was her boyfriend but got killed in the war. I always wondered why she never got married, she is so nice. She also told me that her mother, my grandmother, was a Sioux Indian! I have to think about it more, but I think it is pretty cool.

Well, I have to get some things done. Write and tell me what you are doing when you get a chance.

Love,
Cousin Harold

Next he called Lisa to see about Friday. One of her brothers answered, who knew exactly who he was. She had gone somewhere with her mother. Harold said he would call back after dinner. He knew better than to leave a message with a brother, then wait and wonder if the girl had gotten the message.

He remembered Gloria would be late due to another meeting about what books were appropriate to order for the year. He got an apple and sat down and finished reading *Our Town*. He reread the part where Emily died while giving birth and is allowed to go back to visit her twelfth birthday, before going on. He spent some time sitting there considering her question.

Harold could see her watching the people who can't see her. Then she turns to the Stage master and asks, "Does anyone ever realize their life, I mean every minute of it?"

He replies "No." Then adds, "Saints and poets, maybe, they do some."

He knew at Gilman's he just did what he was supposed to without thinking very much. Most customers were just that, customers, not people to really interact with. They wanted him in his role too, he was sure. You said "Yes, Sir", or "Yes, Ma'am," and got them what they wanted or the best substitute and asked them if there were "Anything else today?" Unless there was something unusual, that was it for about fifty hours a week. "Me clerk, you customer."

He laughed at himself. Sounds like an Indian caricature. He hadn't intended it; he realized he was becoming sensitive to such things since Aunt Gloria's talk with him about his Sioux grandmother. He knew he consciously tried to get every nuance of what she said, and in some cases, didn't say. She seemed so connected to everything.

He knew also that he tried to keep up with Lisa but there was so much in her head and behind the smile. He was sure she didn't mislead him. He just didn't fully understand. One of the guys in his class who rarely dated had said that women had created science fiction so they could read about themselves. Harold considered this rather far-fetched.

He thought about how he liked Peter King but really didn't know him that well yet, but he tried to be very attentive when they talked. He realized he didn't spend much time thinking about his parents. He had to visit home one day soon.

The phone rang and he answered. "Oh, hi Lisa. I was going to call later...Your brother said it was very important? I guess that is what brothers do!...I just asked for you and he said you were out with your mother so I said I would call after dinner ...No, don't hit him or anything, I'm glad you called...Well, due to the parade I get off work about eleven on the Fourth of July and wondered if you had plans...Oh, that's cool that you have a party for the kids, so you get home at the regular time?...How about if we go down towards Harrisburg and get something to eat and then see the fireworks? A customer told me that down toward the Capitol is the best show...How about 6 o'clock? ...Great...Yes, I'll probably watch the parade then come back here and do some chores and get cleaned up...Okay, I hear her in the background. Go snap some beans...Bye."

When Gloria arrived she looked a bit tired.

"Harold, would you get yourself something for dinner? I want to go talk to Peter about the meeting we had tonight." She went back out and even let the screen door slam lightly, something she rarely did.

After eating what he could easily scrounge, Harold walked up the little rise to the garden and stood there watching things grow. In the setting sun he walked up the path into the trees. He walked slowly thinking about Lisa and how attached he was becoming to her and then about the fact that at the end of the summer, both would be heading off to school. He dwelt on it a bit and got nowhere so he tried to get it out of his mind. He continued on through the woods and got to the top of the hill just in time to see the sun go down behind the mountain to the west. The sky brightened as he turned and headed down to Aunt Gloria's.

As he came out of the woods, he looked over towards Peter's house and saw Aunt Gloria and Peter seated talking on the old bench faced away from him. Peter's arm was around

Gloria's shoulders and she leaned against him. Harold's face beamed as he quietly walked to the back door.

The next morning as Harold was having some cereal on his way to work, Aunt Gloria came downstairs.

"Harold, do you have any plans for the Fourth of July?"

"I get off at eleven and thought I would watch the parade then do some chores up here, then when Lisa gets off work we were going out for dinner and then to the fireworks in Harrisburg."

"I know a nice free restaurant with limited seating you could try." Harold looked at her quizzically. Then he got it.

"Peter used to camp a lot and likes to cook out, so we are going to do something and you and Lisa would be welcome. You could leave early enough for the fireworks. We're just going to see what we can from up here."

"I'll call her tonight, but I'm sure that's fine. See you later."

By the time Gloria and Harold had returned home that evening Harold had already talked with Lisa.

"She said she would bake some brownies tonight since she knows you like them, and be glad to eat here tomorrow."

"What a memory. A couple of years ago some girls would come to the library and read to little kids. At the end of the program she brought in brownies and I told her how much I loved them. Be wary Harold, the way to a man's heart..."

"Aunt Gloria, she doesn't need brownies. I think the strawberry-rhubarb pie got me hooked!"

Chapter 18
> Harley Davidson Motorcycle with all its myth and rumble.

19
Fourth of July

Peter was showing Harold how to make a "venison burger" at the stone grill halfway to the garden. He explained that since they were more lean than beef he made them thin and cooked them just through. Otherwise the outside would be too dry and the inside not done enough. Lisa came in the drive in her brown Plymouth. Harold made a mental note to say something to her later about his kidding about a brown car. Peter's Pontiac wagon was a shade of metallic brown. She took a bag, presumably the brownies, into the house where Gloria was.

He and Peter continued at the grill putting on the patties they had made right there from a bowl of ground meat that Gloria had prepared with a little chopped onion and other seasoning.

As Gloria and Lisa came out with some aluminum trays of food, Harold heard almost girlish laughter but knew better than ask what it was about.

After the cookout, Harold and Lisa left in his car and went toward Harrisburg.

"You know there is something cooking with your aunt and Peter, besides venison burgers. When I went in she was getting things ready but just sort of floating in the kitchen. I have known her for years and never saw her like that. What do you think?"

"I agree. I came down the hill the other night and they were on the bench faced away and didn't even see or hear me. They were peacefully lost in their own world. You know I think of Aunt Gloria more like a friend than an aunt. They both lost so much in the war. I hope this works for them. She even went over to talk to Peter when something upset her at the library meeting. She usually kept things to herself and worked on them alone."

They enjoyed watching the fireworks from a parking area on the west bank of the Susquehanna, but enjoyed each other's presence more. Just above Harrisburg they drove up a road to where they might see more distant fireworks, just ending.

As they sat preoccupied with their own fireworks on the high pull-off, Harold became aware of the rap of exhaust pipes with minimal mufflers coming up the hill towards them. He tensed and took his arms from around Lisa. A lowered '50 Ford with no hood ornament, painted in grey prime, pulled in next to him.

"Lock your door," he said as he locked his. His window was open a couple of inches.

Two guys got out and looked in his car. One said, "What are you doin' man and who's your cutie?" He appeared drunk and the second one had a beer bottle in his hand.

"She's my girl. What's that old 'Found on Road Disabled' you're drivin'? Muffler fall off or can it run?" The change of direction caught the drunk off guard.

"Beat that piece of shit 'Garage Man's Companion' any day."

"Not likely. We're just leavin'. Want to head down the road to the highway and run at the light right now, if you got it in that heap?"

"You're on, boy!" They jumped in their Ford and headed down the hill. Harold followed closely.

Lisa held her door handle and seat and said anxiously, "I don't want to race, Harold."

"Don't worry." He focused on his driving. Quickly they were at the stop sign at the main road just north of the light he had referred to. The driver of the Ford peeled out toward the light, throwing some gravel at Harold's car by doing so. Harold let a south-bound car pass, then gunned his car north. He used as much of the acceleration and speed from his Corvette engine as was safe, running up the open road at about seventy for a while, then slowed as he approached some lights and a little town.

"Sorry to scare you, Lisa, but I did not want those drunks up there with you and that was the best I could think of right then."

Lisa slid over and put her hand on his neck and whispered "Thank you," in his ear and kissed him gently as he continued to head home. To himself, he thought, "I guess I have Marion to thank for that exit."

When they returned to Gloria's, there was a light on at Peter's house but no one in sight. They both had to work the next day so they walked to Lisa's car. She leaned against it and they kissed goodnight. His arms around her and she with one at his shoulders and one at his beltline pulling him close. She repeated, "Thank you," and kissed him again, then headed home.

"Fireworks," thought Harold.

They both liked to walk and after the experience with the drunks, the next week, they went up the hill and way in toward the next road from Lisa's house, "for a hike."

They sat together in the hilltop field that once was a pasture but hadn't been used for the two years the farm was for sale.

"Don't let anything ever happen to you, Harold." Lisa said out of the blue as they sat looking at the river and valley below.

"I don't disagree at all, but what make you say that?"

"Just sitting here in the field, with that old tree over there, I got thinking about a movie where they were on a hill, playing around a tree, with fields like this and later on the guy, who was a war correspondent, got killed in Korea."

"Oh, I loved that one. Jennifer Jones and William Holden in 'Love Is A Many Splendored Thing' and then the song! I wrote a report about it for English. It was based on a memoir by a Eurasian woman named Han Suyin. Oh, that is interesting…"

"What do you mean?"

"Remember the main part of the story revolved around her being Chinese and European ancestry and the prejudices and traditions and rules against mixing races. I am going to have to think about it some more now that I know I am part Indian. Funny how a detail changes how you look at something."

"All that stuff, prejudices and that, is so wrong! I don't care a bit who your ancestors were and they were wrong in Hong Kong to have those rules and values. It's like in 'South Pacific' too. 'You have to be taught to hate and fear those whose skin is a different shade…those whose eyes are oddly made.'"

"Fine for you and me, Lisa, and I am glad you feel that way. But so many people just look down on others who are different. I heard two guys talking who come in the hardware store all the time. One has a farm and the other a repair shop. They were talking about busses and integration down South and one guy said, 'They ought to take all those – I won't say his word – Negroes and make black top out of them.' Got a laugh from his friend. Part of me wanted to say something, but the part that wants a job shut me up. Charles has told me how he has had to just shut up some times"

"It's not up to you to change them. Just don't act that way yourself and say what you want about your own ancestry."

"I've been reading about the Sioux and other Indians. Aunt Gloria brought me a couple of books. One cool thing I read about is that sometimes a person might give another one a gift of something that is very important to the giver. The other honors him by accepting it, but owes nothing in return and nothing is expected. Usually we expect the other to give something back. Like at Christmas, your parents give you things and you give them something, except when you're really little."

"Just take care of yourself for me, Harold. F and M will be far enough away. Don't decide to quit and write a book about riding to Mexico on a motorcycle or something, or be a beatnik hitch-hiking or become a war correspondent and get killed. I guess I'm a bit selfish. I want you around."

He turned to her and took her in his arms, kissed her and held her close to him, there in the field full of Queen Anne's lace and daisies.

Chapter 19

> "grey prime": Used for a while until the owner had the inclination for a finished paint job.

> GMC and FORD derogatory names: Garage Man's Companion, Found on Road Disabled.
> With compliments to "Love is a Many Splendored Thing" and "South Pacific," enjoyed then and now. Both dealt with the then-difficult theme of mixed-race marriages.

20

A Splendored Thing

They had taken a picnic dinner including Gloria's Thermos with its several cups, and a nice thick quilt that had seen better days, to sit on.

They headed up their hiking path to the unused pasture of daisies and Queen Anne's lace. It was sort of a celebration. They had met by the side of the road with Lisa's two flat tires exactly forty days before. It was one of those great summer nights before the hottest days of August set in. It was warm, not humid, with enough rain recently that everything felt fresh, but not muddy.

Harold had been reading about Indians. So that no one, especially her brothers, would follow them and sneak up without warning, he asked her to walk below where they liked to go and then circle up to it, so that if someone followed their path through the grasses, Lisa and Harold would see the intruders before being seen. Lisa was amused and thought that would be fun. So they carefully walked across the hill and circled up and back to the little recess from which they liked to watch the river and the sky by the old tree. They spread the quilt and made themselves at home. They both had wanted what then followed.

The next day Lisa pulled into the parking lot at Gilman's just as Harold was checking his oil and about to leave. His eyes lit up with thoughts of the night before and then he got a little nervous, not expecting to see her there.

"Harold, you are the greatest guy in the whole world and I just had to tell you face to face, not on the phone tonight, and especially not with my parents and brothers around." Her words rushed out.

Conscious of being out in a very visible place he took both her hands and held them tightly in his, but did not wrap his arms around her like he wanted to. She squeezed his to tell him she understood. "I was a little worried you might have second thoughts..."

"Just the opposite. I want to tell you something that was on my mind but I couldn't tell you before now. But I can because you are just the opposite. Oh, Harold."

Harold stood there knowing something good was coming, but not having any idea what it was. She was smiling at him. "At the end of last school year, one of my girlfriends, I won't say her name, told me about when she was seeing this guy and it was the first time for them. She said they were out on a deserted road in the woods and got in the back seat of his car. She said he was in so much of a hurry. He kissed her a bit and touched her and then got her panties off and just sort of got on her and pleased himself. She said she had heard stories of how nice it was supposed to be but that it wasn't that way for her at all. He was just in and out and told her how good it was. I was more worried about that than all the strict upbringing I have had. But dear Harold, you were so good to me...."

For the first time he saw her break out in tears and quickly wipe her eyes on her sleeve.

He fumbled out just, "Are you OK?"

The smile was back. "Very much better than OK!" She squeezed his hands again. "I have to run help Dad, but I just had to see you. Call me about eight. We'll talk about other things."

As she turned to leave, Harold got out the word, "Sure!"

21

Cousins

The summer moved along like a placid river, calmly and slowly. For Harold and Lisa and for Gloria and Peter, it was a happy time of love and getting to know each other even better. Each with their own jobs and chores, but spending other time with each other occasionally, like the Fourth of July eating together, but usually leading their own lives.

Harold had gotten off one Sunday by telling Mrs. Gilman very directly that his mother insisted he come for Sunday dinner since she hadn't seen him in so long a time and that she and Harold's father wanted to meet Lisa. Harold and Lisa made the drive in his car and enjoyed a dinner of chicken and mashed potatoes and gravy with lemon pie for dessert. After a pleasant and uneventful time they drove back before dark.

One evening in the quiet flow of the summer, Gloria had told Harold very simply and directly not to worry if she didn't come home that night that she would be at Peter's. Harold was happy for her and not surprised at all.

Harold came into Gloria's drive after work one hot August day. Sitting by the door was a young woman who looked tired and a bit disheveled. Dark hair and eyes. Dark-complexioned, with a pack next to her. Very different in look from Marion though. About twenty, he guessed. He didn't recognize her, but she seemed vaguely familiar nonetheless. He parked and walked over to her.

"Hi. Can I help you?"

"Is this Gloria Eberheart's home?"

"Yes," said Harold. "Are you a friend of hers?"

"I hope to be. She doesn't know me. I am Eva Red Star Sanchez."

"Did you say Red Star?"

"Yes. Do you know the name?"

128

"My grandmother was Carol Red Star. Are you related to her?"

"She was my mother's half-sister, but I don't think Carol ever knew she had a sister. My mother was born when my grandmother, Margaret, was well into her forties."

"I'll have to put this down on paper. This is amazing. That means you are some sort of cousin of mine and Aunt Gloria's."

"That is why I came all this way." About then Gloria came home from work.

After introductions were made again, Gloria said, "Well come in and sit down. You must be tired and hungry." Inside, she cut some bread and cheese and put it on a plate and poured some milk. "Have some while I make dinner and tell us how you came here and found us."

Eva politely took some food and began. "I want to show you something." She opened her pack and took out a folded piece of cardboard holding a piece of old white paper with a drawing on it of a dog, or so it seemed. It was the work of a child. She turned it over and in a readable child's scrawl it said "GLORIA EBERHEART." Gloria looked at it. For the first time, Harold saw her unable to say anything.

"My mother, Eva, got this and some other papers from her mother before her mother died. She was told it came by mail from Carol in about 1927 or 1928, but that things were not well with my grandmother. She had never replied to the letter from her daughter, with this drawing from her granddaughter she had never seen. My mother lives in New Mexico now. She was born in 1919 right after the war. Her father didn't stay around. I think my grandmother had a drinking problem.

"As a teenager, my mother liked to weave and heard that Indians in New Mexico did weaving and somehow got herself down there with her few things and no money during the Depression. She met my father there. He was older than she was. He was Carlos Sanchez, who was mostly Navajo but part Spanish from way back when. He died last year. My mother is

129

thirty-nine now and lives in Los Ojos, where she weaves with a group, up towards the Colorado border. I did pretty well in the Mission School and decided to go east and get a job and go to school and become a teacher. I am going to Philadelphia where the Quakers have an Indian Committee.

I also wrote to one woman named Brinton. She said she would help me get into school and find housing and a job."

"I had heard your father worked for the Pennsylvania Railroad, so I wrote them and told a little lie and said I was looking for my grandfather who worked for them. The office in Philadelphia said he worked in Enola. When I wrote them, they wrote that he had died. I got some money together and used the priest's phone and called the woman who answered the letter and she gave me his last address. So here I am. I hope you don't mind, but besides my mother, you are the only relative I have alive. Well, now there are two of you!"

Harold looked at Gloria who had worked in total silence. She broke her silence to explain to Eva that she had often wondered about her grandmother and knew that her mother had tried to contact her, but never knew if her letters got through. She recounted that when she was in second grade, she had a drawing she had brought home from school. Her teacher had her practice writing her name and then she had proudly put it on the back. She told her mother to send it along when her mother explained to the inquisitive child that she was writing her own mother. They had never heard anything in reply. "I guess you are the reply, Eva! Thank you for coming."

Gloria excused herself and went upstairs to her room, then returned slowly down the stairway. As she came down she looked at an old photo in her hands.

"Eva, this is the only photo I have of my mother. She was sitting where you are, right in front of that window. A man from the railroad visited with us. He was working with my father and had a new camera with a flash attachment on it to take interior photos of trains. I had never seen one. I don't know just why he took it, but I have kept it carefully for years."

"She looks a lot like my mother - the cheekbones, the nose and hair and strong eyes. They looked very much alike, though just half-sisters. Thank you for being here at the end of my journey. Were you an only child? No, I guess not, if Harold's your nephew!"

"I have an older sister, Edie Jenkins, Harold's mother. We are quite different, but I am sure she will be glad to meet you. I am sure you know that some people of mixed ancestry try to 'pass' for various reasons. Edie and her husband had not told Harold of his heritage. Since he is here this summer I just had to. I made a promise long ago that I had to keep."

"Harold, run over to Peter's house and tell him the news and invite him over for dinner for the occasion."

"Peter?" Eva inquired.

"Peter King. He rents a little house from me. But since you are a relative I'll tell you, in the last couple of months he has become more than a tenant. He is the assistant superintendent of schools here and we share a lot in common. But nothing is official, so he rents and we are 'friends.' With his position and mine at the library, we have decided to keep a low profile and see where things go. Some people love to gossip."

As Harold left, he noted that Gloria seemed to like telling another woman about Peter. After a while Harold returned with Peter. They sat down for dinner and the retelling of Eva's story. During dinner, Gloria made it clear that there was plenty of room and invited Eva to stay with them for a while.

The next evening after work, Harold found Eva sitting on the log by the garden and joined her. They chatted about her trip and life while they waited for Gloria. Harold turned and got up when he heard a car and saw Lisa coming in the drive. He walked over to her. Eva got up and looked in her direction.

With less than her usual smile, Lisa said, "Who's she?" She nodded at Eva.

Suddenly Harold realized her thoughts. "I think I see a little green monster flying around. It's okay. She came to see Gloria. She is a cousin from New Mexico."

Her smile back, Lisa told Harold, "I trust you but I guess it is the nature of a woman to protect her territory! But be careful. A problem we Brethren have is marrying second cousins. You are spoken for. So introduce me. I am sure she's interesting."

Relieved, Harold introduced them and almost felt left out of the conversation as the two young women hit it off. Lisa too had thoughts of becoming a teacher. Harold left them to talk and went to do some weeding and hoeing in the garden that he had left undone from the day before.

After a while, Lisa called him. "What do you think of taking Eva on Monday when we go to see your parents for the day? I got it off. I'm sure it would be a surprise for your mother in particular."

"Taking her with us is fine, but I think I may want to tell Mom and Dad first. Mom in particular doesn't deal with new things too well. But either way, what do you say, Eva, want to go and then maybe you can meet your friend in Philadelphia. We can call her, too."

"Thank you both. That would make it much easier for me."

"And Eva can come visit our farm sometime this weekend while you work."

Harold couldn't remember the last time he rode in the back seat of a car. All five were heading down the turnpike in Peter's Safari. Gloria sat in front, Harold behind her, Lisa in the middle and Eva behind Peter. Gloria and Peter were talking. Eva and Lisa chattered along. Eva was quite impressed by the Turnpike. She said almost all the roads at home were sand and gravel. T The road from Santa Fe had been blacktopped some of the way to Los Ojos, partly due to a big government project along the way.

They arrived at about one-thirty, having eaten sandwiches in the car.

Edie greeted Gloria warmly, not having seen her for some time. Peter was properly introduced as tenant and friend who had offered to drive them. Although they had told her in advance, it was a bit of a shock for Edie Jenkins to meet her cousin Eva who looked much more like an Indian than Edie did. It took her awhile to get accustomed to this relative, a perfect stranger.

Peter offered Harold his car so he and Lisa could take Eva to meet Mrs. Brinton, who by good fortune, lived only five miles away.

"Thanks Peter. I'll take good care of it."

"You better," joked Peter, "If you don't, I get yours!"

Mrs. Brinton was very well organized and appeared to have a busy life with her committee work. She greeted them warmly and gave them sodas, and had a packet of materials for Eva all prepared. Eva clearly was not the first to be encouraged in this way.

They were on their way sooner than they expected.

Harold and Lisa decided to show Eva around some of the shops near the "Pike" before going home for dinner and stopped in Green's to get a soda.

Harold was delighted to see that Mr. Green had hired his friend Charles to replace him for the summer. Charles was headed to Morehouse in the fall.

"Hey, Harold!" Charles ran over and they patted each other on the back and shook hands. "I appreciate the good word you put in for me for this job. Who are your friends?"

"This is Lisa Burkholder. She goes to Juniata. We've been seeing each other since June. Lisa, this is my friend Charles White I told you about."

Lisa shook hands politely.

"And who is this?" asked Charles.

"This is Eva Sanchez, my new-found cousin from New Mexico." They shook hands.

The girls left Harold and Charles to talk and went to look at the magazine rack.

"Man, not that it matters to me, but she looks like an Indian. She's your cousin?"

So Harold told his long-time colored friend about learning that his grandmother was a Sioux Indian and how Eva had arrived. Charles was obviously fascinated.

"This is so cool. Maybe you and I are cousins, too!"

Harold looked at him with his quizzical look like some use the word "Huh?"

"I never thought to tell you, but my grandfather from North Carolina was half Cherokee Indian. Neither family had liked the mixing he represented. Neither family had anything to do with the other as he grew up. He came north and met my grandmother from Camden. They moved to Harlem where my mother was born. And I guess all the Indians are somehow related, so maybe we are some sort of cousins!"

Harold patted Charles on the back and said, "That is cool, cousin!" Both laughed. Harold realized that he would have to think about the concept, farfetched as it sounded.

The girls returned to laughter. "What's up?" asked Lisa.

"I just learned Charles is one eighth Cherokee and he just found out I'm one quarter Sioux, so we might be distant cousins!"

Neither girl had any real idea of what was going on.

Both Harold and Charles liked the concept which broke through the societal boundaries neither wanted, but that they had long felt between them.

Dinner was uneventful. The normal day-to-day conversation of events, Peter's job and Eva's meeting with Mrs. Brinton.

Apparently Harold's mother and father had talked privately before the visit. Harold's father shocked him pleasantly when he said in a matter of fact way, "Eva, when you have your paperwork done for Mrs. Brinton, and you are ready to come to the area, you are certainly welcome to stay here in Harold's room until you get other arrangements made."

Eva thanked him, and Gloria said she would see that she got there after Harold left for college. After an early dinner, they returned to Gloria's.

Chapter 21

> Friends Indian Committee: a long-standing committee of The Philadelphia Yearly Meeting of the Religious Society of Friends. Brinton is an old PA Quaker name.
> "second cousins": Inability to have children has resulted among some Anabaptist groups in PA, possibly from limited gene pool.
> The "big government project" refers to "Trinity," the atomic bomb development and the Los Alamos facility begun in 1943.
> Morehouse was the top male Negro school of that time and continues.

22
"Got it Bad"

"How come you almost always wear earrings, Aunt Gloria," Harold asked before turning in one evening.

"How come you don't, Harold? I like earrings."

"Guys don't; well, guys like me don't."

"Sailors used to."

"I give up. I was just curious since you don't usually dress up real fancy, just nice, but you usually wear earrings."

"Joe told me he liked me to wear them, so I do. He never said why. I've gotten to like that one extra thing. When did you say that Lisa is going away?"

"She leaves tomorrow. It's funny, Aunt Gloria, when I was on my way here this June before that accident, I stopped to take some pictures of the Juniata and sat there on the bank and wrote in my journal. I was alone and free and no one knew where I was. Not that you and my parents didn't care, but there was just me. Now with Lisa things have changed so much. We are so close in every way. I know we both have to work and that in the fall we will be apart, but even now I miss her being away for a few days and she doesn't leave until morning. I know that it is really nice that they take the crippled kids away camping for a few days, and I know it is her job and that she loves it, and I want that for her. But part of me feels stretched to where she will be. But I will go to work and do my chores and finish the piece I am writing for college about *Our Town* and still I will miss her."

"You've 'got it bad,' Harold, to paraphrase the song."

While Lisa was away, Harold completed his initial assignment for his writing class. *Realizing Life: Summer Thoughts*

I sat by the Juniata River in June and said to myself as I wrote in my journal, that I was all alone and that no one really knew where I was. At the time I felt everything was going the way it should be. I had done well in high school, was going to college and probably would continue wrestling. My car, which I had worked hard on, was running well. As I sat there I wrote, "things were the way they were supposed to be."

I started "realizing life" almost around the next bend. I realized that we are connected to other people even if we don't know their names.

Two cars hit head on. A medic from the Korean War, only a few years older than I, asked me to help him until the ambulance came. One guy died. I don't know his name. Another guy lived as did a woman and her baby. I don't know their names, but Mike, the medic, and I did what we could, talked over coffee, then parted. I will probably never see him again. But that day is imprinted on my mind and I began to think more about life and part of that life is death.

And I learned about caring for those whose names we don't even know.

I met a hardened girl to whom I gave a ride. Tough and street wise, I learned from her. I also saw that I am more introspective than she. And I am more questioning and interested in what really happens and why.

I worked at a hardware store where I quickly found that the woman was the boss and learned to do what she wanted. But I was there basically for the money and in a certain relationship to the customers. Many times any true interaction with them would not have been a good idea. I am still bothered by the comments of one customer regarding Negroes. One of my best friends is going to Morehouse. But I needed the job so I was quiet. Charles would have told me to be that way to keep the job. He had confided in me how Negroes learned to avoid conflict, saying, "Yes Ma'am" and get by.

Personally, I have been most in touch first with my aunt, and then also with the young woman I am seeing who is away as I write this. Of her I will keep my feelings to myself. My aunt has come through so much pain from a loss in the war and has survived so well that I admire her and listen to her words. She gave me a place to stay this summer to be on my own and work near her home.

I met a man named Peter who also lost a great deal in the war. I admire him as he goes forward leading a worthwhile life. He will not speak of killing or battles. Meeting him and hearing of my aunt's lost love and meeting Mike the medic, I worry about the conflicts I will have over this thing we call war, our way of killing each other with a just name.

And I have thought a lot about a blanket that my aunt has, made in the Southwest long ago. It's a weaving without a border in the design.. I have begun to realize that our lives are woven too, with people and events as the yarn. And I realize that I do not yet comprehend just how the weaving process works. But the unbordered vision becomes more appealing the more I think about it.

Assignment re: Our Town   **Harold Jenkins**

Chapter 22

> "I've got it bad, and that ain't good" from the song by Duke Ellington, 1941.

23

Unfolded Letters

When Harold came home from work Gloria greeted him and said, "There is a poem Peter wrote on my desk. Read it and tell me what you think."

Equinox

The aging war chief sat amid his robes along the wall of his lodge of many years.
Younger children and a few near their time to become men and women sat near.
Smoke drifted up the ceiling hole and curled away into the chilling of the night.
"Grandfather" a young woman respectfully spoke to the chief,
far her elder but not directly related,
"Speak to us of the fire we watch, it's spirit and its ways."
He turned, slightly smiling and began, "Just as the cougar and the buffalo
have different ways and spirits which you will learn as you grow,
So too have fires of brush and twigs and grass and logs,
each their own ways and time and purpose."

He turned a bit and pulled his robe and then continued:
"When we begin our late summer's hunt and our legs carry us easily each day,
and the sun still warms, the earth at night holds heat.
"We quickly gather brush and twigs at hand,
some fast-burning dry cottonwood from down in the hollows;
"a spark comes quickly from the moving fire stick, and the tinder
and flames rise fast to cook the evenings meal.
"Flames linger long enough for stories of the day's hunt to be told,
then quickly turn to coals and ash.

"But the fire before us is not the same. Is it too a good fire?"
A maiden of twelve summers ventured.
"It, too, is a good fire my daughter, but this is the moon
when the deer clash antlers." He looked away, then back,
"This fire took longer to start, the wood more precious, more scarce.
The time, to carry, stack and dry and tend is greater as we approach
the moon when the bear sleeps.
"As all men must change their walk, as have I from when I was war chief,
so too with time we need our lodge fire. Our lodge fire does not flare
like the hunting fire but gives a growing warmth
that lingers even when all is white outside and cold."

*Another spoke: "When do we change fires? How do we know what day
to leave our hunting fires and come and start our lodge fire?
"The Great Spirit has been good to us, my children, by giving a sign:
the moon when day and night rule the sky in equal parts,
but no fixed day when the travelling fire must end or lodge fire begin.
"Do not linger too long by the fast-burning light.*

*As you feel that winter comes as I do in my bones,
go then to the more difficult task of building your lodge fire."
The Chief's Woman now spoke in even tones.
"And you children, go now to your lodges, the night is here."
And as the youths began to go
"It is the autumn's night and time my man lay down beside his fire."*   **Peter**

Later that evening Harold sat outside with Aunt Gloria. She asked if he had read the poem. He replied, "I really like him and think you were wise to wait to find Peter. I remember reading that someone said, 'Alone is better than the wrong one.' I don't know if you saw me come down the hill that night you came home from the library upset and let the door slam and went to Peter's. He had his arm around you. Since then I thought he was the right one." Gloria blushed as much as a darker complexioned person could, but smiled.

"I just asked you about the poem."

"Remember I told you about missing the meaning of 'the woods are lovely, dark and deep, but I have promises to keep and miles to go before I sleep' in Miss Rose's class? Well, I resolved then to look at everything I read carefully and see what is really there. You and Peter are building the lodge fire with 'growing warmth' not just a 'hunting fire.' Guess I shouldn't say 'not just' about a hunting fire, should I?"

"No, and if you do, you better not let Lisa hear you!" replied Gloria, regaining composure. "When does she get back?"

"Tomorrow night. The four days seem so much longer."

"By the way, Mrs. Jackson is going to stop by with some books and information from the library board meeting I missed the Monday we went to Philadelphia. She is the one I think I told you about; very nice, but pleasantly nosy and a devout gossip.

Remember: 'Mr. King' rents from me. That is all, if the subject ever comes up. Feel free to excuse yourself if you want. I will tell her all about you and F and M, and if she mentions Peter I will say, 'Isn't it nice he did something with his life after losing a leg using his Veteran's educational benefits rather than only going on disability.' That will give her something nice to talk about."

"Got the message, Aunt Gloria!"

Earlier while reading the poem, Harold had also found a carbon copy of a letter to Peter which was left near the poem. He knew that Gloria sort of let him find out things. He was not sure if she wanted him to read both the poem and the letter, so he did not mention reading it.

August 1958

Dear Peter,

I decided to write to you while you are away at the seminar to tell you what you know already and some that you don't know. That is the hard part and why I choose to write.

First, you have become so special in my life. I never thought I would again feel about anyone the way I do about you. I have told you and shown you but I just wanted you to have it from me in writing, so to speak. With you I have found something I lost fourteen years ago and never thought I would have again: A person who truly cares about me and about whom I care with all my heart. There have been other men for whom I had a passing interest but they lacked the depth and intensity that you have. I do not compare you to them. There is no comparison. You are you.

I am sure you have an idea though about my loss. You don't miss much. I am sure Harold has told you at least a little. By the way, I will share the poem "Equinox" with him as you said I could but I don't expect him to comment on the Indian part. Right to building a lodge fire!

I am glad you have talked with him so much. Obviously he is very smart but talking to an older, wiser man can only benefit him. I don't think there is much depth to his conversations with his father. So I am sure you have heard of Joe Schmidt.

We met when I was seventeen at the Harrisburg Farm show. From then on there was no one else for me. He will always have a place in my heart and you must know that. But his place does not diminish yours. You would have liked him. He grew up on a farm but he was present where ever he was. We were in New York one time and we met some people who were very different than around here, but he got along just fine. He treated me so gently and well that I knew I was far better off than my various girlfriends with their guys.

But you know only too well the war came along and like you, he had to go. I wished he hadn't had to go but I knew he had to. He regarded the nazis as a blot on his German ancestry and the world (he wouldn't even give them a capital letter, so I won't.) Since he could run any sort of equipment the Army made him an engineer.

They landed at Anzio, Italy in January of '44 probably when you were on your way to England to go on shore at Normandy. A couple of days later he was killed. I didn't know for a couple of months. His family never told me since they rejected me for my Sioux ancestry. An English medic wrote me and sent Joe's last two letters to me. If I hadn't had Dad to care for, I don't know how I could have stood the loss. But I did.

I don't mean that you are another Joe. No, you are you: you are my dear Peter King. And I am a totally different person than I was when Joe died. I have read so much and talked with people at the library so much that I am really a different person now. And had he lived, he would probably be different too. I guess that he would have used the GI Bill to study something like you did. Hopefully, we would have married and had children and grown old together.

But that was not to be. And I lost him. I just wanted to tell you myself. And I don't want you to be my new Joe. That can't be and shouldn't be. I have found what I lost, that is, a love I am sure of. I have only one request of you and I will lay my loss to rest. Joe's name for me was "Glory." I like my name Gloria. Please call me Gloria.

Love,
Gloria

24

Lisa's Back

It had only been a few days, but Harold could hardly wait for Lisa's call that she had promised to make as soon as she got home. He felt like going outside in the hot August evening, but kept himself downstairs reading the last of the books about Indians that Aunt Gloria had brought him. It wasn't the most exciting book he had ever read. It told of the various tribes and nations and where they had been located. The only thing that really got him interested was the brief part about Tecumseh and how he tried to unite the Shawnee, Cherokee and Northern tribes and of his defeat when his British allies abandoned him. He had been named for the comet that passed at his birth, "Panther in the Sky."

The phone rang next to him and he grabbed it on the first ring. It was Mrs. Jackson from the library. "Is this Mr. King?" she asked. Harold quickly explained who he was and that Mr. King rented next door and he thought he was away at a seminar. Then she explained she was calling Gloria about the library and Harold explained she would be home later, and that he thought she was shopping. He was glad to get off the phone to wait for Lisa.

A half hour later it rang again and he answered on the second ring. "Hi. I am so glad to hear your voice!...Sure, I'll be up in a half hour if that is what you want...Bye."

Harold drove up the hill, thinking of how many times now he had headed up or Lisa down to Aunt Gloria's. It had become the norm for them to see each other as much as their schedules allowed. He pulled into the drive and parked near the barn. He saw Lisa coming out to meet him. She didn't have her brightest smile. Maybe she had been discussing something with her mother, he thought.

She walked his way and said, "Let's go for a little walk." He took her hand and they headed up the path they usually took and after a little, he asked, "Are you okay? I am really glad to see you."

"Harold, of course I am glad to see you too, but I need to talk to you. I should have gotten my period the day I left and I haven't gotten it yet and I am usually very regular. I'm worried."

Harold paused a bit and wasn't sure quite what to say. He continued to hold her hand and said what he could think. "I am not sure what to say. I really don't know much about these things. I know we took the right precautions. Whatever happens, I am with you. Tell me what you are thinking."

Tears came to her eyes. She put her arms around him and put her head on his shoulder and they stood there for a while up among the trees, on that warm night, out of sight and out of hearing of her family on the farm.

"My mind is going in different directions at once. I don't want to be pregnant. If I am, I am glad it is you. I want to continue with school. I'm not ready to be a mother. The camping trip was draining. The kids had fun, but twenty-four hours a day uses a lot of energy, especially with their handicaps. I hope it is just that I have been so keyed up that has made me late. Part of me says we shouldn't have and part of me wants you even more. I don't like being confused."

"Well, whatever, if you want to get married, I would be happy with that. I'm here for you, Lisa."

She held him a little tighter and they continued just to stand there among the trees, the August sky still bright in the early evening.

After some quiet time, Lisa spoke. "Harold, I better go in. I am so tired from the trip. I'll be able to deal with things better after a night's sleep and I have tomorrow off." They kissed and walked back to his car.

Harold drove down to Aunt Gloria's, confused and bothered but not knowing anything else to do. He did some chores and turned in, sleeping fitfully, worrying about Lisa.

Just before he left in the morning for Gilman's, the phone rang. "Hello...Hi Lisa...So everything's fine?...I woke up worrying about you several times last night...Great...See you tonight after work...Bye."

That afternoon when he got the mail after work, his mind still on Lisa, and their possible change that had not come about, he was glad to find a letter from his young cousin Couly.

Dear Harold,

You are as much a gossip as a girl! But do you really think Aunt Gloria is interested in Peter? She is so nice, he better be a really good guy. Keep me informed Cousin Gossip!

And how are things going with your new girlfriend Lisa? You wouldn't have mentioned her if you weren't serious. It is funny you mention Miss Bessie. She has started talking more with me about things that are important, not just which dress I should wear today and stuff like that. She seems to know all about everything that is going on with lunch counters and all that. She seems really happy about it. She says that all things come in time. She asked me to remember "I know in my heart, for our world, that good overcomes bad. Positive is stronger than negative."

I know that for her and other colored people that things have been awful bad at times. But still she says good overcomes bad. I think I shall remember that. Everything is good for me and I hope it will stay that way.

So you are an Indian now! Do you still dress the same? I am just kidding. I guess you talk the same too, so I guess it is not such a big deal.

Do you think I should keep a journal? I don't want everybody to read stuff I write. Do you keep yours locked up? What's the difference between a journal and a diary?

I guess I will have to mail this since if I put it in a bottle it will go the wrong way if I throw it in the Bay!

Love,
Couly

P.S. Say hi to Lisa for me!!!!

25

Songs in the Rain

"Whenever we're in a car we always have whatever music is on, but I never asked you: what do you really like, Lisa?"

"That's funny; I was just listening to the new album of *The Music Man* and thinking about Marian the Librarian and your Aunt Gloria. She sure is being nice to Eva. Taking her to work every day and giving her stuff to do so she knows how to run a library, then giving her books to read before she goes off to school. When she came up to my house last weekend when you were working she was just so happy with everything."

"She talks a good bit at night but has given herself reading homework she does almost every night. We all get along fine."

"I'm sure she will work out fine when she gets to Philadelphia. But I was going to say, in *The Music Man*, they never really told much about Marian's life. I think it is nice that your aunt talks to you now. And also to Peter. But I know that it has to be kept quiet. I have known her for years, but I always called her Miss Eberheart and never really knew anything about her except that she is a real nice librarian who would talk with me. But never about herself. But I like good musicals much more than most popular stuff; I mean some are just plain dumb."

"Like what do you mean?"

"Oh, let me think. It's hard to think about something you didn't want to remember like *Great Balls of Fire*. Big deal, but who cares? Now *Twilight Time* wasn't bad and I really liked *Catch a Falling Star* that Perry Como sang. Did you know he was from Pennsylvania?

"Yeah, I heard that. Funny, looking at the rain tonight, I was just thinking about it. 'Catch a falling star and put it in your pocket, save it for a rainy day...'"

"Got a real star, you, Harold, but sunny days are fine too!" She kissed him and snuggled closer on the seat looking out at the rain. They had been thinking of going for a "picnic" on their hill, but had to put it off. Instead of walking in the rain, they had driven up the hill and turned left twice to go around to the neighboring vacant farm and driven into the drive, out of sight of all. The warm August showers beat on the car.

"Did you hear that Van Cliburn play? Talk about what I like. My roommate Clara, who we met in Lemoyne, just got the record. I think it is so neat that he won over in Russia; beats arguing and fighting with them. But he was smart to play a great Russian piece for the finals. And he got a Russian to conduct with him when he recorded."

"I heard it on the radio at Charles' house just before I came out here. His mother plays piano, usually jazz, but made us listen to it when it came on that day. Pretty neat."

"And I like the Kingston Trio, too. I think they will catch on and you know I love *South Pacific*. Why do you ask?"

"Lisa, dear Lisa, don't you know I want to know all about you? I didn't come out here to find you. I didn't even come out here to get a job. But I got the job and some guy dropped junk on the road. My lucky day."

"Hey, I got two flat tires. Well I guess you are worth two flat tires when I think about it. In some countries I might be worth two camels, so I guess you are worth two flat tires!" She held tight to Harold's arm.

"Ever think about how things happen? Like how we met. If I had met you in the store or at the library I wonder what would have happened."

"You mean like is there a big plan somewhere, is everything all figured out and we play the parts, or do we just happen into things?"

"Exactly; sometimes, I think about it. When I was in church one time I remember hearing from the Old Testament, 'What is man that thou art mindful of him?' Is anyone or thing mindful."

"I mean why are things the way they are? Not just history. But like you finding out that your grandmother was an Indian.

Look at all that is involved in why you didn't find out 'til now and why you did find out."

"Like what?"

"Well your parents probably felt it was easier for you to grow up like everybody else and then you said Gloria made a promise to Joe to tell you if no one else did due to how his family treated her."

"I have a question for you that I thought about on the way home from Philadelphia with Eva. Would you still feel the same way about me if I were part colored?"

"But you aren't. I finally got what you and Charles thought was so funny about him saying you were cousins. You guys are such good friends but since he is colored and you are white, there is always something separating you. So when you found you were both part Indian it gave you something in common and he called it being cousins and you both really liked it."

"You don't miss much, do you Lisa! But you didn't answer my question."

"I can't really, because you aren't and if you were we probably would never have met and you would have been different. I don't mean I would be prejudiced, but there aren't any colored families around here so you wouldn't have been driving up the hill in the first place. It just isn't a real question and I can't answer it. Please don't get mad 'cause I didn't say 'Of course.' You get the truth out of me, Harold. And that is I am lucky I met you, that you are, my sweet, smart, gentle Harold."

Abruptly changing the subject she said, "Did I ever tell you that I think you have a really good car? I meant to tell you after you fooled those drunks to protect me then really took off. You have to be pretty smart to do what you did with this car."

This was the first time Lisa had said anything about his car. The shift in conversation let him get off the unanswerable question he had posed about color and he just said, "Thanks. I did work hard on it."

Lisa shifted back to music. "I like that new one, *Volare* – 'let's fly way up to the stars.'"

"I like it too. That's how I feel with you. And I remember too saying 'fireworks' to myself when we kissed, back in July."

"Fireworks will do just fine for me too right now," she said as she turned into his arms.

"By the way, my cousin Couly said to say hello to you."

After some time with no conversation, Harold lamented.

"Lisa, in a way I wish you were pregnant. Not that it would be a good idea, and I'll be careful every time, but I will miss you so much when we have to go to our two schools. I know, we will write and see each other often, but I guess I want a reason to just stay together."

"Do you really want to talk right now? I feel so warm and nice here with you with the rain outside. I feel the same. Shhhh. Hold me close."

August 16, 1958

I don't know how I am going to concentrate on my work this fall. I have to keep my scholarship, but Lisa will be on my mind all the time. I have to figure something out. Maybe I should say "we" have to figure something out since she says she feels the same. This can't be just a summer romance. I never felt anything like this before. She is it for life as far as I am concerned. I've gotten used to her being a bit assertive and I even like it when she drives. No one I ever went with is as smart as is. She really understood about me and Charles. And she is right that the answer to some questions has to be "I can't answer that question." I guess that some of the times I have thought that I don't like unanswered questions, I was dealing with questions that could not be answered.

Chapter 25

> In 1958, *The Music Man* and *South Pacific* were hit albums. Hit pop tunes included *Great Balls of Fire, Witch Doctor, Twilight Time, Catch a Falling Star,* and *Volare.*

> Van Cliburn returned to a ticker tape parade in NYC after winning the First Annual Tchaikovsky competition in Moscow.

> Psalms 8:4 "What is man, that thou art mindful of him?"

26
Peter's Back

August 19, 1958

Aunt Gloria has been really fidgety the last day or so. I'm glad Peter gets back tomorrow from that conference at Penn State. She was telling me I "got it bad." Speak for yourself, Aunt Gloria, as they say! But I am really happy for her. Peter understands how much she lost in the war. I don't think people like me can really feel what it means to suffer a big loss like they each have. I'm glad I haven't. I don't even want to think or write about it.

But even seeing that guy whose name I don't even know, with part of his head missing, stays with me. Imagine if he had been a buddy of mine that I really knew. We have to stop having wars. Aren't we smarter than that? Can't they solve things other ways? But Hitler, I don't know. I guess I would have shot him if I were over there and had the chance. But all those other Germans, were they really that bad? Sure dumb anyway, to get led along by him. I wonder what would have happened if people had not cooperated like Gandhi said. It would have been hard to stand up knowing pretty well you would be shot. I hope we keep out of that stuff and find another way. Ike doesn't like wars.

This guy Kennedy some people want for 1960 got sunk in a boat and his brother got killed. I don't think he will be for a war. And Ike's VP, Nixon, has probably learned from Ike. Someone said he is a Quaker. Maybe it will be peaceful awhile.

*I have lots to learn in college, but I really don't
know what! That is, what I want to be or do. How
do I know what to take? One course at a time.*

Aunt Gloria almost ran in from work and asked, "Harold, will
you run over to Peter's and invite him for dinner while I go clean
up? I got so dirty cleaning out and shelving books today. Then
pick some beans that look good. Thanks."

Harold obeyed her gentle command. He knew she wanted
to look nice when Peter saw her for the first time in two weeks.
Apparently Peter had arrived that afternoon when they were
at work. He headed over, invited Peter, explained to him why
he thought Aunt Gloria had not come over herself, to Peter's
amusement, then got a bunch of beans.

He glanced out the window and saw Peter coming so Harold
excused himself and went to the garden to do some hoeing.
Leave them alone for a bit, he thought with a smile.

"Gloria tells me you read my poem and you think we are
building a 'lodge fire', Harold," Peter said when Harold returned.

"Well if you read it symbolically, I guess so."

"Well, then you know we expect it to take some time to get it
right and make it last. I don't mean that a hunting fire, as I called
it, can't grow into a lodge fire, I hope you realize."

"That is nice of you to say, but Lisa and I don't have to be
bound by your analogy. That is your poem, and I like it, but I
think a lot about the older blanket of Aunt Gloria's and I don't
like the idea of having borders around me, not of my choosing.
Lisa and I have talked a lot and plan for things to continue
between us and have said we hope things go right for you and
Aunt Gloria, but we don't plan to have others tell us how we
have to do things, even those we like, like you."

"Well put, Harold. You speak better than some of the
teachers at the conference. One woman quoted something I
liked. '...man should know his own self and recognize the parts
that lead to loftiness or lowliness, glory or abasement, wealth or

poverty' or something like that. She said it was from a religion from Iran that she was studying. I am glad you two feel you can know yourselves without others running things."

Gloria added, "I think you know that Peter and I don't try to set your borders. Sure we are glad to talk. In fact I want to tell you something and please tell Lisa. Peter and I are very serious about each other."

Harold smiled as if to say, "Do you really have to tell me." Aunt Gloria continued, "But the reason we are keeping it to ourselves for now is so that we won't be under lots of pressure of all kinds. This area is really a small town. Everyone talks about everyone else's business and then about how they should be doing whatever it is and then someone self-delegates to tell them. It is nice in a way. If you dial the wrong phone number you probably know the person you got and can talk for ten minutes anyway. Until we have everything the way we want, we can do without others planning a marriage or what church we should go to and speculating on children and whether I will give up my job, which I won't, and all sorts of things that really are only our business."

"I know what you mean. When I first met Lisa I was used to everyone knowing who I was at home and so when she wouldn't take the help I wanted to give, I was a bit miffed, but realized that I really wasn't known in her world. Glad I didn't get too upset. Then one day Mrs. Jackson called from the library and asked if I were 'Mr. King' when I answered the phone. I'm sure it would have been the start of good gossip if it had been Peter, but he would be too smart to have answered. I hear enough at the hardware store. I understand and so does Lisa. We keep some things to ourselves too..."

"There is more, too, Harold," Peter added, "Gloria and I have each spent a lot of the last years living alone. We have each had people in our lives for short times. But when you get used to living alone you get in certain patterns and get used to making your decisions without taking into account what someone else wants or plans. Even without community pressure or gossip we plan to go slowly. You won't push someone into your own mold if you care about them. All sorts of things matter. Gloria is much more of an early bird than I am. But we appreciate your letting us keep our privacy as we get to know each other. I just rent from her."

"He's a real good tenant!" added Gloria putting an arm around Peter's neck.

The conversation at dinner went to a recounting of the seminar and life at Penn State. Then about a Seneca fellow Peter had met from northern Pennsylvania.

Then Peter said, "I'll tell you a tale with a good point that I heard when I worked among the Chippewa..."

They talked through dinner until Harold offered to do the dishes and Peter and Gloria went for a walk. Harold did not hear her come in that night.

Chapter 26

> "man should know his own self" from writings of the Baha'i.

27

Goodbye Harold

Harold was surprised when at about two forty-five on his last day to work, a Sunday, Mr. Gilman called him over to his office area. He handed Harold his check for the week through four o'clock that day but said, "You must have things to do so you can finish what you are doing and leave at three. Thanks very much for your work this summer. Mrs. Gilman said just make sure you know your pots from now on, City Boy! Think about coming back next summer. Gossip is, you have interests other than your Aunt Gloria in the area. I hear that new school administrator is living up at her house."

"Well, Mr. King rents a little house from Aunt Gloria. He seems like a real nice guy. A real hero from the war."

"Oh, just rents? Well that's nice. I'm sure he makes himself useful if she needs anything, all alone with you leaving, but she's been by herself so long, since your Grandpop died."

Harold shook Mr. Gilman's hand, put his check in his pocket and finished putting away some tools. He waved as he went out the door for the last time and then drove up to Aunt Gloria's.

He pulled in the drive and overhead was a sign that said "GOODBYE HAROLD." Out by the grill he saw Peter and Lisa, her four brothers, and her father, Aaron Burkholder. Then Eva came out with a large pot. He guessed Esther Burkholder and Aunt Gloria would be in the kitchen.

He parked where he usually did and Lisa came over and kissed him lightly right in front of everyone - not their norm!

"Surprise, Harold! Since you have to leave in the morning, we all got together to say goodbye. Actually it was your aunt's and my mother's idea I think. They seem to like you." They walked hand-in-hand towards the grill area.

Lisa's fifteen year old brother, James, who often answered the phone, spoke first. "Harold, we decided you are okay and you got a cool car too! You sure beat that guy she liked year before last!" The younger ones nodded affirmatively with their usual grins.

Lisa gave James as dirty a look as she could muster. Then Aaron Burkholder stepped over. "Got to say that I like you. Work hard, get home when you are supposed to. We'll see. I think you are also the kind of young man who knows responsibility and will do the right thing if he is ever faced with a tough decision. Hope school goes well for you. Often wondered what college would be like, but from what Lisa tells me, it's better I stayed with farming"

"Thank you sir, I plan to work real hard." Harold gulped slightly not knowing quite what, if anything, to read into his words. They shook his hands and turned to see what Peter was doing. He was adjusting the fire a bit so that the large pot of baked beans could sit by the coals to warm. Eva had added some fresh onion and catsup to the canned variety for more flavor.

Aaron continued, "We could call this a Harold roast, like when they get together to talk about some famous person, since we have all been talking about you while we waited for you to arrive. It was real nice of Mr. Gilman to let you off early. We invited him and his wife, but he said he had to join her at a church dinner tonight. But Harold, he said you had worked hard enough to get an hour off with pay. He let you get here earlier, so that is a big compliment, considering the source!"

Aaron Burkholder patted him on the back. "If you knew Gil as long as I have, you would know what a big deal that is!"

Harold looked around, and really felt on the spot being the center of so much attention. About then, Aunt Gloria and Esther Burkholder came out with covered trays. There was corn that had been freshly shucked and Gloria had defrosted enough venison steaks for everyone to have plenty. Esther went back in and brought out lemonade and poured for all.

Peter said "To our departing young man, Harold!" in a form of a toast and raised his lemonade. Others raised theirs except the youngest Burkholder who was already drinking his.

"Speech, Harold," added Gloria. Harold paused, again at a loss for words, something he noticed had happened to him more than once this summer.

"Let's see, 'Four score and seven years ago...'"

"That one's taken," chimed in Lisa, getting into the joviality of things.

"Really, I don't know what to say. I think it is cool to have a little party but it is for everybody together, not just me. You are the neat people who let me have such a great summer. Let's just talk and eat and be glad we're here and the weather isn't rainy."

Harold and Lisa sat on a bench near Eva. Harold spoke.

"Really this should be for you. You came a lot further, and still have a lot to do to get into school." Lisa nodded affirmatively.

Eva replied, "No, you all made me feel like I had joined the party when I got here and when you took me to Philadelphia and made such good arrangements for me. That was my party. I have a lot to learn for my pueblo and lots of training to become a teacher so I can go back to my people and be a help to them. I have so much to do before I deserve a party."

Esther and Gloria were talking over their lemonades. Esther said, "I like him very much, but I hope they finish college before getting married and having children. We were only nineteen and eighteen when we were married and Lisa arrived when I was nineteen. Taking care of kids and the house has been more than half of my life. But I do want her to find a nice young man who will be good to her like Aaron is to me. Is it your nephew? I do not know. She will find such joy in her children."

Gloria replied, "It seems with each new year that we have so many new choices to make, not just lots of choices we have always had, but the world offers new ones we never thought of before. I never planned my life. I met Joe, Mom was gone, the war came. Joe was gone, then Dad. So I am here in the house I love with good neighbors and a secure job. But I still can't see tomorrow clearly, but I know it will come. I don't pray for a life to enjoy. I just try to enjoy life as it comes. And what will be next for my dear Harold, I don't know. He will do well in college. I told him the other day, 'You got it bad' about Lisa. Got his big smile. He said it was the strawberry-rhubarb pie she baked, it seems like so long ago! By the way, her apple pie smells great."

"She even picked the apples herself next door where the farm has been for sale so long. They aren't ripe, but she insisted on going up there for them. The kids selling the farm want a lot for it but they don't want the farm for themselves. She and Harold love to picnic up there. I remember when Aaron and I used to go on picnics when we were very young." And then Esther said with a funny smile, "Maybe I better not remember too much!"

Peter and Eva were in an animated conversation. She was very interested in his teaching on the Chippewa reservation in Minnesota. She explained that she was very sure that she would return to New Mexico after getting her degree and teach in the reservations or pueblos there. "We have to get educated. It is great and important to keep the old language and understand our traditions. But this is a big world we live in. We have to face it even if we just look out from home. Many Navajos have radios now. One day many will have TV sets. TV's only work near a place like Albuquerque now, but soon we will be watching a much bigger world than ours. We need education to make sense of it. And teaching is what I should do for my people. Actually I have read a lot to kids in the lower grades. I love to see them when they finally 'get it.'

"I hope Harold doesn't forget the Oglala in him. I look Indian. He doesn't. He can do what he wants. But that's for him to choose. Ever think how much we get to choose, even when we do have limits, like our looks?"

Peter replied, "Yes, I know too well. I recently repeated to Harold a tale told to me among the Chippewa, but I bet it has many variations all over since there is so much truth to it. I have heard it as two wolves but also an eagle and a wolf. But that one ranks the eagle over the wolf. I prefer this version since I like wolves. 'One evening, while sitting by their camp fire, a wise Indian told his grandson about great battles. One was going on inside himself. Another battle was inside his little grandson. He told him that a battle rages within each of us. It is between two wolves. One is evil: of anger, envy, sorrow, regret, greed, arrogance, self-pity, guilt, resentment, inferiority, lies, false pride, superiority and desire. While the other is good: of joy, peace, love, hope, patience, serenity, humility, kindness, empathy, generosity, truth and compassion. 'Which wolf wins?' asked the grandson. Grandfather simply replied, 'The one I feed.'"

"I will remember that for my students." Eva commented.

Harold and Lisa spent most of their time talking together with their friends. Aaron approached Gloria fairly soon after eating and explained that they must go do the evening chores. "But we will excuse Lisa from her chores, if Harold will be so very kind as to bring her home."

Harold immediately said of course he would, then saw the smile on Aaron's face and realized humor in his phrasing.

James spoke up. "Can us guys have the cans from the beans to make stuff, Miss Eberheart?"

Guessing, she said, "I bet you are going to get some string and make a telephone." A smile greeted her and James ran into the kitchen and returned with his treasures. He and the three younger boys climbed in the back of the pickup.

Esther got in the car with Aaron and they headed home.

Lisa and Harold talked with Gloria and Peter and Eva, then since Lisa had to work in the morning, Harold took her home. They were talked out. They sat in the car for a while, arms around each other, where Harold usually turned his car around, out of sight by the barn. Knowing the family had seen them come in, they kissed good night. Harold reminded her, not really needing to, "I'll be up in the morning before you go to work."

Aunt Gloria was waiting for him when he came in, which was a bit unusual, since all summer she had left him to himself.

"I'm going to see Lisa in the morning before I leave. I don't really want to go."

"Harold, remember. F and M is about two hours from Juniata. Your only worry is keeping decent grades. But that isn't why I waited for you. I saw the books you read about Indian heritage, so I am sure you will understand something." She reached down to the chair next to her and picked up the carefully folded, unbordered blanket. "This is for you."

Harold looked with surprise but as he had learned of Indian custom, simply accepted the treasured gift with, "Thank you," as Gloria turned and went out the door to Peter's.

28
Unbordered

Early Monday morning Harold arrived at Lisa's house just before she had to go to work. "This is the first time I've hated to drive up this hill! Leaving you and heading for home and then F and M is something I don't want to do. We've talked about it before but it is on my mind." She took his hands. "Thanks for saying it. Though I knew you wouldn't say something like 'Well it was a great summer, maybe we'll meet again someday.'" Not worrying whether brothers or parents were watching, they kissed goodbye. Harold forced himself to turn for his car.

She stood there on the step by the door. Her smile faded and returned as if to make sure he remembered her that way. They planned to write and then visit as soon as school allowed. She waved as he got in his car. Then he got out and returned with his camera. "I don't have a picture of you. Just stand there by the door," he said and took a picture of the smiling girl. "I will send you one of my freshman photos they said they're going to take."

He returned to the car, started it and began to drive away when he heard a terrible noise from under and behind his car. Lisa came down from the porch. Harold got out to check and heard her brothers beside the barn laughing loudly, almost in tears. He looked behind the car. The cans from the beans from the party the night before were carefully tied on strings hooked to the rear bumper of his car. Taped to the trunk were two signs on bag paper. One said, **"HAROLD LOVES LISA"**. The other, **"GONNA GET MARRIED"**.

Harold and Lisa just stood there slightly red-faced but also enjoying the carefully planned prank. The boys had pretty much left them alone all summer so it wasn't so bad. Harold unhooked the cans and threw them in the general direction of the laughing boys. Then he carefully untaped the signs. He put **"GONNA GET MARRIED"** in his car and said, "I'll remember with this!"

Then he gave her **"HAROLD LOVES LISA"** and said, "So you don't forget!" She kissed him again and blew him another kiss as he went down the drive. The smile left as he turned down the road. He did not see her little tears form.

There was almost no traffic on the Turnpike as he headed east. His mind wandered. A small part of him looked forward to getting started at F. and M. College had always been a goal. But Lisa was foremost on his mind as he thought and worried. Would they continue? Would the separation and being around other decent and intelligent people diminish the attraction they had for each other? Would she find someone else, or just decide he wasn't quite the right one despite their closeness and intimacy? As he had often written, he didn't like unanswered or unanswerable questions, and he had lots of them. He tried to get these worries out of his mind for now. He wondered if he should mention his Sioux ancestry at college. He decided not to make a big deal of it and just wait and see. He wandered in his thoughts back to the image of the dead guy partly out of the car. It still bothered him. Pointless, like Joe's death. And then he thought of the strong character, Marion, strong but not as reflective as he or Lisa. He thought back to all he had learned from Aunt Gloria, and Peter too. He knew he did not ever want to be faced with the decision of having to go to war.

Then he turned and looked on the seat next to him at the unbordered blanket Aunt Gloria had given to him. In June Harold had preferred Aunt Gloria's newer Navajo blanket with a border. But the events of the summer led him now to understand and prefer her well-used, unbordered one. Gloria realized this and gave it to him. "I remember the off-white walls in the dorm room at F. and M. I'll hang it on one of them".

An Afterword from Harold's friend Willard McKay

As I wrote, this is not really a novel that I have put together here. A weaving of stories and memories and letters would be more accurate.

I hope you have read it slowly. Obviously, it was not meant as a fast-paced action book. I believe we are bound to look at our lives and our pasts and the events that happen, and to examine them. We can then see how our experiences may benefit ourselves and others around us in the broader world.

"If I am not for myself, who will be for me? But if I am for myself alone, what am I? And if not now, when?" These words come to us over the centuries from the wise Babylonian Rabbi Hillel, who taught in Jerusalem before Jesus. They are valid for more than just one group of people.

Wars have impacted so many lives and continue to do so. Going forward from tragedy and injury is surely a quality to be respected and admired.

Death appears unexpectedly from time to time in our lives. We have no ready answers or explanations.

Harold was lucky to have his Aunt Gloria. I have also been fortunate to know insightful people. We should not only gain for ourselves, but also for those we come in contact with who are open to growth as we ourselves have grown. We cannot run the lives of others. Perhaps we touch them some. We can do our best to follow the guideline, either from Hippocrates, or the Roman physician, Galen, "First, do no harm."

We do not have to see eye-to-eye with those we learn from. Harold gained insight from Marion, though he had problems with her outlook.

Hopefully we can all find another with whom to build a fire, of whatever kind their time of life allows. But this is difficult either for those who examine, or do not examine their lives. Some say it is just luck. I am not averse to that. Someone said, "Given a choice of skill or luck, take luck!"

Where do we go from here? I go my way and you go yours, but we have met in these pages about Harold's life and hopefully we have gained by looking at this unbordered weaving.

And then the unanswered question appears. Can we look back at our own particular weavings, and if not satisfied, take the time to unravel some? When the Navajo received whole blankets from the East which they found unsatisfactory, they took them apart for the wool and rewove blankets to their liking. They liked the wool, not the weaving.

So we ask, can we alter or "reweave" our lives more satisfactorily than what has been woven before? Some will curse their fates. Others will believe they deserve the good fortune that their weavings brought. I hope I go forward using the wool that life affords me, like Tennyson's Ulysses, "to strive, to seek, to find, and not to yield."

Willard McKay

Thanks to my sister, Mermie Karger, for her support while I worked on this book and to Ronni Miller of Write It Out for her workshops.